Apprehensive Hearts

Tony Varnis

D1279926

ISBN:1724606735
ISBN-13:9781724606730

DEDICATION

To all the closet romantics, would be lovers, and
uncertain suitors out there, I dedicate this little tale

Tony Varnis

ACKNOWLEDGMENTS

Cover designed using
Cover Creator

Cover art by

Ebooklaunch.com

1:INTRODUCTION

The Administration Building of Mackenzie Academy is an impressive sight. Gray stone, two stories high with two faux bastions on the front corners. As you ascend the stone steps it would be easy to imagine a volley of musketry catching an unwelcome guest in a cross fire. A bronze plaque on the cornerstone proudly proclaims "HEADQUARTERS 1891".

The academy was originally a military school named in honor of Ranald Mackenzie, a lesser known hero of the Civil and Indian wars. In the nineteen twenties, the school abandoned the military theme, becoming an upscale prep school. The Admin Building is one of many reminders, however, of its past. On this day in the early dusk, the lights shining warmly through the windows were a stark contrast to the cold bleakness outside.

It was December twentieth, 1998, the end of the last day of classes at the Mackenzie Academy, the start of the Christmas break. John Drake had just finished dropping off some papers at the administration office and left the building. He was an American Literature professor at the small private boarding school and was looking forward to two weeks of leisure over the holidays. He had nothing to do and was glad of it.

Once outside he inhaled deeply, he loved the feel of cold air in his lungs; it seemed to have a cleansing, invigorating effect on him. Walking down the steps of the Administration building, he crossed the narrow roadway, and began walking across the large open field known as the Common. Originally the Common was the Parade Ground, but soon after the school dropped the martial theme and became a prep school the now superfluous Parade Ground was rechristened The Common. In better weather it served the students as a kind of park; a gathering place where touch football was played in the fall, snowballs were tossed around in the winter, baseballs in the spring, and pep rallies were held whenever they were warranted. All the older buildings on campus had been built surrounding it with castellated facades. It was all rather picturesque. Every brochure the school put out displayed at least one image of The Common.

On this night in the early darkness of December, the Common was bereft of both its military bearing and its park like atmosphere. Empty and quiet, with some light snow flurries falling, blown by the wind, melting as soon as they hit the grass, it had a lonely peaceful feel to it. John liked it this way. The same way the cold air seemed to refresh his lungs, this night time stroll home seemed to clear his mind.

He crossed the imaginary line between the campus and the town, two blocks away from his apartment. The houses along the street were decorated gaily for Christmas and the cheering secular lights were a stark contrast to the solemn spiritual darkness of the Common. He liked this too. Walking down the wet street he was already trying to decide what he was going to drink when he got there. Beer was good for a long haul drinking session, it was his usual choice, and wine seemed more holiday like, but tonight he was in the mood for a brandy or two. It seemed like that kind of a night.

Arriving at the house, he went up on the front porch, checked his mailbox and emptied it. Then he went inside, on the stairs leading up to his apartment he saw a package. His landlady must have placed it there earlier, it was too large for his box. The mailman must have left it on the porch floor and Mrs. Smiltrisky probably brought it in when she took in her mail. Picking it up, he saw the return address, it was from Rita. Suddenly he had a nervous feeling in his chest. He went up the stairs to his apartment and set it down on the kitchen table.

He was actually reluctant to open it. He took a TV dinner out of the freezer and microwaved it. He ate his meal, ignoring the package. He wasn't sure why, he just knew there was something about it that unsettled him; he wished it had never come.

Finishing his meal, he went to the closet where he kept his liquor on a top shelf. He paused for a moment before bringing down a bottle of applejack. He decided to drink an American innovation tonight. He sat sipping it in his living room watching the yuletide specials on TV. The alcohol had a steadying effect on him. When he finished the first he decided it was time to see what Rita had sent him. Even then, he thought to himself it's a Christmas present; if it's wrapped in holiday paper, he shouldn't open it until Christmas Eve at the earliest.

When he ripped off the brown paper outer wrapping he saw he was out of luck; No gift wrapping, just a corrugated cardboard box. He opened one end and slid out its contents. Amid wadded up newspaper there was a framed picture. A homemade Christmas card was wedged into it; he removed it and read it. There was a frowning Santa Clause on the face of it and the heading, "Poor Santa, he only comes once a year", then when he opened it, it stated "And that's only down the chimney!" Below that in handwritten script, "I finished this about a month ago and I thought you should have it, Luv, Rita."

He looked at the picture, it was Carol. Done with colored pencil, it was an almost perfect portrait of her. Rita had left nothing out. Though softened, the laugh lines and small crow's feet on her face were clearly visible. Even the darker streaks in her blonde hair were included. Rita had captured her roommate's beauty flawlessly, almost as if she understood that it was these very imperfections that had attracted him to Carol in the first place. He always felt it was easy for a young woman to be attractive, but the ones whose looks held into their forties, they were the honest beauties, character lines and all. Then, of course, there was the smile. It was the genuine one, not the one she presented to the world at large, but the one that said she was truly happy, the one he'd fallen in love with.

He poured himself another drink, took the portrait into the living room and set it on top of the television. As he sat there drinking he tried to watch the screen, but his eyes kept moving to the portrait. There was Carol, smiling at him, head slightly tipped, shoulder length hair down with the ever present bangs on her forehead, the way he'd seen her so many times in their brief time together. It was almost as if she were in the room with him. The picture was like a ghost haunting him.

After the third drink, he decided he had to do something about it. Rita had opened the door, welcoming him in; there could be no other reason for her to have sent him the portrait. He felt he had to walk through it. He thought about the possibility of driving to Manhattan that night, but rejected it. By the time he got there it would be late, he had nowhere to stay, plus he was tired, too tired to make the drive especially after drinking. It would have to wait until morning. He had one more drink, and finishing it, he picked up the picture and walked into his bedroom setting it on the dresser.

"Well, Carol honey, tomorrow's going to be a big day and you don't even know anything's about to happen." Then he added in a lower voice, "I hope I'm not going to be wasting both our time."

He went to bed and slept fitfully that night, constantly waking up and thinking about what he had to do in the morning; what he should do. In the early pre-dawn he gave it up and got out of bed. Getting out his suitcase, he started to pack for a two day stay. He was pretty indecisive about what to take, placing clothes in, then replacing them.

He was equally uncertain about going at all. He and Carol had parted company on bad terms last August and he wasn't sure what type of reception he would get. He hoped the months had softened her anger, hoped he could express himself properly, and, most importantly, hoped she would even listen to him. He also felt, however, that Rita had sent him the picture for a reason, that she knew or sensed something about her friend and the situation. He had to find out. If Carol slammed the door in his face, welcomed him with open arms, or was just indifferent to him didn't matter, at least he would know.

Finally he finished packing. There was much to do, it had all seemed so simple last night. He made himself some breakfast, trying to figure out when would be a good time to call Curt. He hoped to impose on Curt and his family to let him sleep in the spare bedroom of their apartment for a couple of days. There was something fitting in that, it was Curt who had introduced him to Rita last summer; that was what had started this whole thing.

He called Curt, catching him before he left for his office. He quickly explained he was coming to town for a few days and needed a place to stay. Curt had unhesitatingly offered the spare room for as long as he needed it. Then he went downstairs to let Mrs. Smiltrisky know he would be gone to have her take in his mail and the morning newspaper. It was Christmas, he felt he couldn't go empty handed.

Curt was easy, he could grab a bottle of Drambuie from his closet and wrap it. He would have to stop at a mall to get something for Curt's wife and daughter, and of course something for Rita and Carol. Hopefully, whatever mall he stopped at would have one of those kiosks where they did gift wrapping.

Later that morning, shopping done, he boarded the bus to the city. He'd decided against driving himself, he was simply too tired thanks to the restless night he'd had. Even driving to an Amtrak terminal might have been pressing him. The bus seemed like the best move. He could get some rest and be in the Port Authority building sometime that afternoon. Picking out a seat he settled in, hoping he wasn't embarking on a fool's errand. The bus pulled out, he relaxed, looking out the window as the town passed by and thought back to the previous summer, about Carol and what a strange time it had been.

It had all began when he'd decided to take a course at the New School, it hadn't been all that important, but it was an excuse to spend a couple of months in Manhattan. He'd always been fond of the city, not fond enough to live there permanently but he wanted more than a weekend visit. So, the idea of picking up a few credits in literature and spending a couple of months there seemed to be a natural. It was Curt who arranged for him to sublet an apartment in his building for the summer. It was also Curt and his wife, Marion, who took him to the party.

It was actually more of a gathering than a party. Held in a small avant-garde gallery in the village, it was touted as a chance to meet undiscovered artists and fellow art fanciers.

"A chance to rub elbows with some of the real Bohemians," Curt had kidded him, "the McCoys, the ones who live for their art; unlike the pseudo-nonconformists who hide out in upstate prep schools."

"I'm still a free spirit, sometimes I wear a turtleneck to class instead of a shirt and tie. And, hey, I don't even own a tweed coat with leather patches on the elbow. These thing get you talked about out at Mackenzie, I'll have you know."

"Real rugged individualist," Curt laughed. "Twenty five years ago you'd have laughed at guys like us."

"Still do," he replied, "it's just that now the

laughter is directed inward."

It was a nice affair. The gallery was filled with paintings by local artists, there was a small buffet table set up, filled with deli meats, cheese, and wine. There was a good crowd, patrons of the arts, so to speak, coming and going, constantly replenishing itself. Curt and Marion seemed to know a lot of them. At one point while they conversed with another couple, John wandered off on his own.

Looking at paintings, wine in hand, he paused in front of one of a small lighthouse. Steel girders rose behind the red structure. He smiled to himself; it was the "little red lighthouse" of children's storybook fame. He stood trying to remember how the story went.

"Do you like it?"

He turned and looked. A woman was smiling back. Light brown eyes, chestnut hair below the shoulders, a short sleeved frilly blouse that accentuated her full bust, John couldn't help being attracted to her.

"Yeah, it's nice. It is THE little red lighthouse, isn't it?"

"Yes it is. You really know your kiddie stories." She paused, "Want to buy it?"

"No, I don't really want to decorate my walls with childhood memories. I was never that much into the story, even as a kid."

"Fair enough, what sort of thing do you like?"

"Guess I would have to say landscapes. Pictures of real things, real places, not that the lighthouse isn't real, but a view of it from across the river would have been more to my liking."

"I see," she pointed to a picture on the nearby partition, "maybe something like that?"

He looked over at it; it was a snowscape of what he assumed was Central Park at dusk. It really was impressive, so was the price tag, however."

"That's really is good. I couldn't afford it, but it's great."

"Thanks, that's one of mine too."

"You mean you did it or you own it?"

"Both, I guess." She held out her hand, "Rita Bowers, starving artist, and you're?"

"John Drake," he shook her hand, "aging English teacher. I hope I didn't say anything insulting about the lighthouse picture, I didn't realize...I thought you were a sales person."

"No, no insult. I only brought it because Andre

said it might sell with the tourist crowd, because of the story."

"So, you make your living as a painter, that's interesting."

"No, I make a few bucks as a painter; I make my living as a stripper." She saw the look of surprise on his face. "Hey, don't be so shocked. I'm an artist; I made a few extra dollars posing for other artists, often in the nude. It's not that big a stretch from sitting motionless totally naked to shaking things up in a pair of abbreviated underpants in front of a crowd. Are you going to go prudish on me?"

"No, not at all; it's just that you kind of took me by surprise."

"Well, I'm sorry about that. But tell me John Drake, aging English teacher, what's your story? You don't seem like some tourist who wondered in because you're trying to soak up some local atmosphere."

"Not that much to tell, two years at a local junior college, then I came here for two years at NYU and got my BA in American Lit. I had dreams of being a writer."

"Didn't work?"

"Not really, after a lot of long, hard work, all I

had to show for it was some nice rejection notices. I decided I was wasting my time, got my masters, then took a job at a private prep school upstate. Sort of like George Bernard Shaw said, 'those who can, do; those who can't, teach'."

"That quote always seemed kind of cynical to me, maybe because I had some good teachers."

"No, it's not really: it's not the put down that most people think. Do you follow baseball at all?" She shook her head. "Well, most of the really great players, hall of famers, made second rate managers. On the other hand, most of the legendary managers were just ham and eggers as players. Failure is a great teacher, I can see talent in my students and when I see it I try and do what I can to encourage it. Now, I've made my rant and tried to justify my decisions, let's move on."

"Sure, now you say you like landscapes, I like doing street scenes and views of the city, do you think they might qualify?"

"Probably, but I have to be honest. This summer is costing me enough as it is, I don't know if I can afford to spend money on artwork; even if I do like it."

"How long are you in town for anyway?"

"Two months, I'm taking a course at the New School. I also want to attend a few writer's seminars

I know about."

"So the dream isn't totally dead, then?"
"No, hope springs eternal and all that jazz."
Rita smiled at him, then looked around.

"Well, John Drake, it's starting to get a little boring here. I don't think I'm going to sell much, and if anybody wants to buy, Andre or one of his people will take care of it. So, if you'd really like to see some of my work, I live within walking distance, come on up and I'll show you my etchings."

"You talked me into it." He wondered if she always invited men who she'd just met up to her apartment. It seemed like a questionable practice, however he chose to flatter himself by thinking she thought he was special. The logical part of his mind said if she was an exotic dancer, she'd probably developed a sixth sense about men and besides that she could probably handle herself if things got out of hand. He thought that perhaps he was the one taking the risk. Looking at her he decided that if that was true, it was worth it.

She disappeared into the back and came out with a large satchel type purse. Gesturing for him to follow she went over to the buffet table and started to make a large pastrami on rye with provolone cheese. John assumed she was hungry and wanted a bite before leaving. She turned and handed him the sandwich and proceeded to assemble another.

"Ah, Rita, I'm not really hungry. I already had…" he was cut short when she looked at him curiously, with a funny smirk. Then he saw her pull a plastic bag out of her purse. Then he understood.

"My roommate was supposed to come with me tonight, but she was tired and fell asleep. I have to take something home for her. Yeah, Andre knows we do it, but he doesn't like to see it. We are starving artists after all. Now this he might not like." With that she reached out took an unopened bottle of wine from the table and slipped it into her bag. "Now my fellow partner in crime, let us depart."

It was a longer walk than he'd expected, but it was enjoyable. In addition to attractive, Rita was witty and intelligent. By the time they reached her building he had the feeling they were old friends, not two people who'd only met forty five minutes earlier. It was an older building, a remnant of old New York, in a neighborhood on the East Side that had survived the urban renewal projects of the mid-twentieth century unscathed and had as yet avoided the current trend of urban gentrification. Depending on how you looked at it, it was either a quaint relic of the old tenement days, or a slum.

Three flights up, they entered her apartment. It too was old style tenement; three rooms, kitchen area on one end, bathroom partitioned off of that, living area in the middle, and a closed door to the front room, he assumed the bedroom. The living room was furnished with a hodge-podge of battered second hand furniture; a couch that had seen better days, a coffee table that looked as if it had seen service as a work bench at one time, and two wooden rockers, heavily coated in green enamel paint. The walls were festooned with her canvases, some finished others not. An easel stood in the corner holding a work in progress.

"Kind of a mess, isn't it?"
"No," he replied diplomatically, "there's a difference between clutter and mess. A small apartment fills up quickly, especially when you're working out of it."

"That's true, we have a storage area down in the basement, but it's pretty damp down there. I can't store my work there safely." She was in the kitchen area, stashing her booty in the refrigerator. Looking over the refrigerator door, she called out, "Sit down, make yourself comfortable."

Sitting down, he looked at the pictures on the wall. He saw what she meant; there was a preponderance of city scenes. They were quite good, if he'd been looking to purchase art there were several he would have been glad to have. One in particular, a scene of Times Square back in the days when the Camels cigarette billboard was still there, blowing smoke rings out over Broadway.

Rita came back in, two glasses of wine in her hands and a binder under her arm. Carefully she set down first one glass and then the other on the coffee table, then sat down next to him and opened the binder.

"I try to take a photo of most everything I finish and have it blown up. Kind of a record of everything I've ever done. I thought you might like to see them. It's not quite the same as the real things, but it'll give you an idea of what I do."

"Sounds good, but I have to ask you about that," he gestured to the Times Square picture. "I don't think you're old enough to remember the Camels billboard."

"You're right, but there are still a lot of old postcards of it around. I found a good one and basically copied it. Did you ever see it?"

"Yes, when I was a kid. We'd come to the city for a visit, I thought it was like the eighth wonder of the word."

"Cool, did I do it justice?"

"Oh yeah, at least as well as I remember."
She got up and went to where some smaller canvasses were leaning against the wall. Tipping them forward one at a time until she found the one she was looking for. She pulled it out and came back to the couch.

"If you liked that one, you might find this interesting." She held it up in front of him, a small painting of Jack Dempsey's old restaurant on Broadway.

Good God, yes. I actually ate there a couple of times when I was going to NYU. It was expensive, but I was a big fight fan in those days, the chance to see a legend like Dempsey was too much to pass up."

"Did you ever see him?"

"Yeah, shook his hand once. He was in his seventies, but I swear, grabbing his hand was like grabbing a chunk of tempered steel. I couldn't help but think what it must have been like to get hit with it in his youth. There was a mural on the wall of him hammering Jess Willard into the ropes to win the title with that same hand. I really got a kick out of it."

"Interesting, I've got some pictures of other nostalgic Times Square paintings I've done. They sell well with the tourists. Pictures of the old stores, Bonds and places like that."

She began flipping through the binder to find them. He heard the door to the bedroom open behind them then a voice.

"Hi guys." He turned, looking over his shoulder. A woman wearing sweatpants and a sleeveless tee shirt walked across the room, not seeming to notice or care that there was a strange man in the apartment. She was medium height and thin. Her blond hair was pulled back in a ponytail. Appearing to be in her mid-forties, she was fairly attractive. This was the first time he saw Carol. Rita turned around on the couch.

"Hi hon, there's a couple of pastrami sandwiches in the reefer, and I copped a bottle of bubbly for us."

"You're a lifesaver, I'm starving."

"Oh by the by, this is Johnny Drake, John, meet Carol, my roommate."

"Hey Johnny," she said pausing, then looked at Rita. "Fellow artist or a fan?"

"Neither, failed writer."

"Oh," she looked at him, tipping her head. For the first time he noticed her odd one sided half smile. "Have you written anything I might not have read?"

"Anything you haven't read, I probably wrote."

Her smile widened, looking less lopsided. She winked at him and started to walk towards the kitchen.

"Ya gotta give him credit for honesty," Rita called after her.

Carol stopped in her tracks, pivoting 180 degrees on the balls of her feet.

"Better yet, he can laugh about it." Then she reversed the 180 and proceeded to the refrigerator.

While he continued to look through the binder with Rita, Carol came back with a sandwich in one hand and what appeared to be a glass of club soda in the other. She stopped behind them, bent down and nudged his shoulder with her elbow.

"Nice meeting you Hemingway, keep up the good work."

John turned and watched as she walked into the bedroom and closed the door behind her. When he turned back to look at the binder he saw Rita, leaning forward, her elbows on her knees, looking up at him with an open mouthed smile.

"Your roommate seems like an interesting girl."

"Yes, she is and I can see she's made an impression on you." She sat upright, leaning back, still looking at him, smiling, "Do you want me to get her to come back out?"

"No," he felt slightly awkward now, "no, let her enjoy her sandwich in peace."

"You're sure? She probably just didn't want to intrude, you know in case anything was going to happen."

"No, that's all right." He wasn't exactly sure how to respond to that, so he added tentatively. "I, ah, didn't know anything might happen."

"Anything is possible," she said good naturedly, "not now of course; not tonight. The night belongs to Carol, seized by her cameo appearance."

"Sorry, I didn't mean anything, I...I don't know what I did, but I hope I didn't insult you."

"No, not at all, and you didn't do anything really, I just saw the look in your eye when Carol walked through. I'm thinking you're more than just a little interested in her. If you'd like to go out with her some night, I'll talk to her and see how she feels about it."

Now he was openly embarrassed. Rita's bluntness had taken him completely by surprise, leaving him uncomfortable, slightly confused, and perhaps a little intimidated.

"Sounds like Junior High School, you're going to ask her in Home Room if she likes me."

"Yes," she laughed, "it does, but these things have to be done somehow, and I don't think you're going to do it on your own."

"Naw, it's all right, thanks though. It all seems silly somehow."

"OK, 'Hemingway', whatever you say. I'll give you my number in case you change your mind. Now, back my work. Since you liked the Dempsey's painting, I've got some other things you might like."

She got up and went over to a bookcase on the far wall and pulled out another binder. She came back over and set it down on the coffee table. Opening it up he saw it held more photographs of her paintings. These all seemed to be scenes of Manhattan landmarks; the flatiron building, the battery, Father Duffy's statue, and others.

"More postcard type things, like I said, they are popular with the sightseers. The good thing is I have the photos copied, stick them in cardboard frames and Andre sells them at the gallery. It's a lot cheaper than buying the actual painting. I could do that with the Dempsey's one if you like."

"There's an idea. Do you mind if I think it over?"

"Up to you."

She got up, went over to the phone stand and wrote something down on a slip of paper. Coming back over, she held the paper out to him.

"My number, let me know when you decide; about either the picture or..." she nodded towards the bedroom door, "fair lady."

The evening ended as simply as that. Rita let him use the phone to call a cab, then went downstairs with him to wait. She claimed she'd never seen a cab in her neighborhood and didn't want to miss it. As they waited, making small talk, she suddenly looked at him.

"You should really think about Carol if you're interested, she's got a lot to offer. She comes with a lot of baggage though; she's been hurt and doesn't need any more pain."

"You seem bound and determined to push us together. I have to wonder why."

"You seem to be a nice guy. She's a friend and I'd like to see her happy, even if it's just for the summer, so it just feels like a natural. So why not go out sometime and see? It might be a good fit. All I ask is don't play her; she may seem leather tough on the outside, but inside it's like she's silly putty. It's like her heart and soul have been thrown into a blender. Think about it though, unless I've just scared you off."

"We'll see," he responded as his cab pulled up.

"Sounds fair," she quickly kissed him on the

cheek. "Now you take care, and if we don't see each other again, it was nice meeting you; Ciao."

He turned to say good bye, but she was already walking through the doorway into the building.

Slightly bewildered, he turned and went to the cab. He couldn't help but wonder about what a peculiar evening it had been.

2: INFATUATION

For the next two days, John kept thinking about that night. He wondered if he should buy the painting or not; he wasn't sure if he really wanted it. He was also thinking about Carol and whether he should call Rita. It didn't make sense to him that he would be attracted to a woman he'd only seen for a couple of minutes, but he was. He tried to understand what Rita had seen that night that made her so sure he was interested in her roommate. He wondered if he really was interested or if it was just a thought that Rita had put into his mind. Then he decided he was wondering too much. That evening he picked up the phone and dialed Rita's number. After several rings he heard her familiar voice.

"Hello?"

"Rita, it's John Drake, from the other night."

"Yes, John, what's up?"

"I've been thinking about that Dempsey's painting, I can't spend the money for the painting, but I would like a photograph of it, like you said."

"Oh sure, not a problem. Let me check at the gallery to see if we have any copies made already. If we do, you can get it any time you like, if not, it'll take a couple of days. Anything else?"

"Yeah, I've been thinking about what you said about Carol."

"Yes and…"

"I think I might like to take her out, you know, get to know her a little better. I was just wondering if you think she'd go."

"Probably would, I don't see why not." Then in a distracted tone, "John, just wait a minute please."

He heard the sound of the receiver being set down, followed by silence. After a short wait, a different voice spoke.

"Hello?"

"Hi, this Carol?"

"Yes it is."

"It's John Drake, I was at your apartment the other night with Rita."

"Yes I remember. How are you?"

"Fine, good," it occurred to him Rita hadn't talked to her at all; instead she'd thrown them together on the phone cold turkey. "Look, I know we only met for a few minutes, but I kind of thought maybe we could, ah, you know, see each other again? Maybe, uh, over dinner or something?"

He heard a funny sound on the phone, then Carol's voice heavily muffled. She'd apparently placed her hand over the mouthpiece to speak to Rita, however he could make out her words, sounding distant but distinct.

"It's cute, he's stammering."

John felt a surge of humiliation wash through his brain. He actually wanted to hang up, or take his offer back. He knew, though, that would just make it all worse. He tried to make his voice sound as light hearted as he could.

"Yes I am."

"Huh?" The grunted response was in normal volume.

"Yes, I was stammering." Then in a low voice, almost a whisper, "Carol, I could hear you."

There was a short period of dead silence before she answered.

"Oh God, John, I didn't mean anything, please, I wasn't trying to offend, I just thought it was kind of sweet." It was her turn to search for words, "It's just that it's been a long time since anyone was nervous about asking me out. Don't be mad, I didn't mean anything."

"OK," he felt as if he was back on equal

footing with her, if not in control. "I'm not mad, but you still haven't answered the question."

"Yes, of course, I'd like to have dinner with you. You have any day or time in mind?"

"Free Saturday night?"

"I am."

"How about around seven?"

"I'll be waiting. Any idea about where we'll be going. Just so I know how to dress."
"Depends on what you like. You're not a vegetarian or vegan or something, are you?"
"No, not at all."

"Good, I feel like hitting a steak house. A strip steak and a couple of beers sound good to me. How about you?"

"I like steak, don't get it that often, so yes. Sounds real good to me."

"Well that's it then. You don't have to dress up too much to go to one."

"I'll be ready at seven then, and please, if I insulted you before, I'm really sorry."

"Don't worry, it's ancient history, I'm well over it. I'll see you Saturday."

Saturday night he climbed up the stairs of their building and approached the apartment door. For some reason he was uneasy, possibly because in his brief dealings with them both women appeared to be unpredictable. He didn't know what to expect, had not a clue. While this added a certain excitement to it all, it was also slightly unnerving.

He rang the bell, seconds later the door opened as far as the security chain would allow. Carol glanced out at him through the crack between the door and the jam.

"Just a sec," she said, then closed the door enough to unhook the chain. She swung it open. "Come on in for a moment. I'm just putting on the finishing touches."

It was the first real look he had of her. There was tiredness about her eyes that he hadn't noticed at their previous meeting. Her smile was the type one gives at a complaint desk, anxious and tentative. He realized she was as unsure of herself as he was. This put them on even terms, somewhere inside he began to relax, his self-assurance returning.

"Finishing touches? I don't see where you need any; you're looking pretty good to me."

"Oh, thanks, that's sweet." Her smile returned to a more natural state, more genuine and less tense.

"Trust me though, I'm at an age where I need all the help I can get."

"I think you're being a little hard on yourself, but if it makes you feel better, take your time, there's no need to rush."

It was one of those statements that sounded better in his head than it did when he spoke it. He meant it to be charming, but it sounded to him to be somewhat condescending. He hoped she took it in the spirit it was intended. Then he decided he was over-thinking the whole thing. The phrase "just be natural" ran through his head. He decided to stop worrying and just be himself.

He sat down on the sofa and waited while she disappeared into the bedroom. It was a brief reprieve, giving him time to regroup. He had hoped Rita would be there to act as an intermediary between him and this woman who he didn't know at all, to help smooth things over. But then he remembered the way she'd thrown them together without warning on the phone. Apparently Rita believed in the sink or swim principle, just toss you into deep water and let you figure out what to do.

Perhaps she was right, both he and Carol were adults and should be able to handle themselves without interference. She was probably right. Finally Carol emerged from the bedroom. To be honest, he didn't see any difference in her. He had no idea what the finishing touches she'd applied were, but again, if she felt she'd needed them and they set her mind at ease, it was well worth the wait. He was already developing a certain fondness for her. He found this surprising and somewhat confusing, while always outwardly polite, he wasn't one to take to people this quickly.

"Sorry to have kept you waiting."

"No problem, it was worth it. Now, somebody recommended a steak place that's not too far from here, within walking distance, long walking distance, but I figured it was better than taking a cab or the subway uptown or me trying to find a place to park my car. We could drive somewhere if you don't want to walk."

"Oh no, it's a good night for a stroll. I'm used to walking, actually I kind of like it."
"You're sure you don't mind? I know all women's shoes aren't good for strolling in."

"No problem here, these are pretty comfortable."

So they set out, Carol was right; it was a good night for a walk. Neither too warm nor too cool, it was just comfortable. Moving through the city blocks, John had a Deja vu feeling; a flashback to his days at NYU when he walked many of these same streets. He was also intensely aware of the woman at his side, the scent of her perfume, the sound of her heels hitting the pavement as they walked. He couldn't help but wonder what she was thinking.

"Where's Rita tonight, having a big night on the town?"

"No, she's working. Friday and Saturday nights are her big nights, the week end crowd."

"Oh, you mean dancing?"

"Yeah, but we're pretty honest about it; we're strippers."

"Oh, you too?" She nodded her answer. "I didn't know. Weekends aren't big for you?"

"Not really, I mostly pick up some time in the afternoons. The prime time I leave for the younger, prettier ones like Rita. It's a different, smaller crowd during the day. They don't mind if the girls are a little older, a little shop worn. In fact, I think some prefer it."

"Well, you're not really that old, what's the problem?"

"In that business, I'm an antique, a relic of past glory. Rita's actually kind of old for prime time too, but she has that body that a lot of guys go for; kind of lush and full breasted. And her personality seems to come across too, that helps. I think she kind of enjoys it."

"And you don't?"

"Not really, it's just a job. It's a way to pay some bills, that's all."

"Are you an artist too?"

"No, I came to New York twenty some years ago to become an actress. That didn't work out too well, but I stayed on."

"That's interesting, no success at all?"

"No, not especially. I went to a lot of cattle calls and did manage to get into the chorus line of a couple shows that didn't last very long. It just wasn't in the cards."

He felt himself growing close to this strange woman. He didn't understand it, but he had an urge to put his arm around her, to hold her, to reassure her she wasn't so old, to give her some explanation as to why she didn't make it as an actress. But it was too soon for that, and he didn't have any answers anyway.

They walked the rest of the way making only small talk; mostly about the weather and how much Manhattan had changed down through the years and about how much Manhattan hadn't changed down through the years. John noted how odd it was that one place could change so much yet remain essentially the same. Then he glanced at Carol and thought to himself that perhaps it's the same with people, perhaps inside she was the same innocent girl who'd come to the city with dreams of stardom. He really wanted to find out.

At the restaurant, seated across the table from her, John had an opportunity to study Carol. He saw once again the tiredness in her eyes and also saw there was more to it than that. Her whole general countenance seemed to be one of someone who has been beaten down by life; world weary. He understood why she had referred to herself as shop worn. Despite all that, she still had an attractive face, one that showed character. Actually he found her more interesting because of it.

They ordered drinks, beer for him and wine for her. Then as the studied the menus she lowered hers and looked at him.

"Look, you should know, Rita and I usually order heavy on dinner dates so we can take the leftovers home."

He continued studying the menu almost as if he didn't hear her.

"There's a twenty four ounce strip steak on the menu that looks pretty good," he remarked casually.

"So, you don't mind? I don't want to take advantage of the situation."

He looked at her and realized this was a woman who'd probably been taken advantage of often in her lifetime, and wasn't willing to do the same to others. The character he'd seen in her face was showing itself. He'd have been willing to buy her ten steaks if she wanted them.

"Hey, if you want the steak, go ahead and order it. Once you do, it's yours, do with it what you want. It's none of my business"

It seemed to him to be harsh statement, even though he hadn't intended it to be. He had been trying to be flip but now was afraid he had come off as cynical or even patronizing. He looked at her, smiled and winked an eye, hoping that that would take any unintended edge off his words. He had the feeling he used to get as a teenager, when he would struggle around girls trying to get every word right, afraid even the wrong inflection would give them the impression he was a jerk.

She, however, returned his smile with one of her own. Looking dead into his eyes, her smile was actually quite beautiful. Open mouthed, showing her upper teeth, it had lost that lopsided look he'd noticed previously. It also put him at ease, at that moment he felt they'd become friends. He took a deep breath and exhaled. He could now relax with her and be himself; he could only hope she felt the same way.

As they sat waiting for their dinners, John

decided he wanted to know more about her. He'd had enough of the chit chat.

"So tell me, when you came to be an actress, was there a specific genre you were interested in? You know, musicals, comedy, drama, or didn't it matter?"

"No, I was game for anything. I could sing a bit and had taken dance lessons when I was a kid, but I would have taken anything. You know how it is when you're young, you think anything is possible. I was no exception."

"Yeah, I can relate to that."

"That's right; you wanted to be a writer. Tell me how that went."

"About the same as you, I spent a couple of years trying to write, finished a novel; that was the start of my rejection slip collection. Had a couple of short stories published in some college quarterlies, a couple of articles in some very small magazines. I gave it up as a lost cause. I couldn't even get an agent."

"Well, we have that in common, I mean I did get an agent, but he wasn't worth a good God damn. He kind of hinted I could sleep my way to the top. Once he got me in bed a couple of times, he moved on to the next wanna' be starlet. I more or less got pimped out to a few of his contacts that he wanted favors from."

"Damn, that was one rough lesson."

"Yeah, unfortunately I didn't learn from it. What's the old cliché' about learn from your mistakes or you're condemned to repeat them? I was a slow learner."

Their conversation was interrupted when their food arrived, but he was haunted by her last words. He remembered Rita's warning that Carol came with baggage, that she was damaged, literally a soiled dove. He was beginning to understand, and oddly, the damage made her more endearing to him.

"Oh God," she remarked looking at the slab of meat in front of her, "it's the size of a small roast. I feel guilty for ordering it."

"Don't worry about it, I know how it works, remember, I'm the guy who helped Rita swipe a couple of pastrami sandwiches and a bottle of champagne the other night. Enjoy it."

"Are you sure you don't want to take some home with you?"

"No, do you think when I finish this," he tapped the sixteen ounce streak in front of him with his knife, "I'm still going to want more? Besides, on a first date, a guy will do anything to impress a girl."

"If you put it that way," she never finished the statement, merely cut into her steak and started eating.

Their conversation during the meal was sparse, consisting of the usual comments about the quality of the food or which side orders were best. John couldn't help looking up occasionally to watch her eat. One time, while he was trying to steal a glance, she looked up at him. Their eyes met and she gave a shy closed mouth smile, then quickly looked down at her plate as if embarrassed. Though neither one realized it, at that moment his heart belonged to her. Things between them would never be quite the same.

Later, when they left the restaurant, as they walked down the street John reached down and took her hand. She looked over at him and flashed the smile. Then quickly she sidestepped, playfully bumping into him.

"Taking liberties there, aren't you buddy?" she teased him.

"Damned right," he laughed.

"What kind of a girl do you think I am?"

"The kind that I desperately want to take liberties with."

"OK, just wanted to know." With that she

jostled him a second time.

"You in a rush to get home?" he asked her
suddenly, "I was thinking maybe we could go
somewhere else and do something. I'm not sure
what, a movie or just a couple of drinks somewhere
where we could talk."

"I like the talking idea. I know a place not too
far from my building. It's nothing fancy, just a
neighborhood place, but it's nice."

"Sounds good to me, if you recommend it."

The bar was exactly what she said it was; just
what you would expect from a neighborhood place.
Long and relatively narrow, the bar on one side with
a low freestanding partition running part way down
the other, hiding some small tables from view.
Down the far end, past the partition, were several
booths. The bar was busy; all but a few stools were
occupied as were a couple of the booths.

The bartender was a short heavy set man
wearing a white short sleeved shirt and matching
apron. The collar of his shirt was unbuttoned and a
clip-on bow tie was hanging loosely from one lapel.
He looked over-worked and unfriendly. Seeing
Carol standing at an open spot at the bar, he came
over. Like many New Yorkers, his miserable
demeanor hid a basically friendly nature.

"Hiya kid, what's doin'?"

"Hi Joe, just dropped in with my friend John for a few drinks."

Joe leaned across the bar, arm extended, offering his hand. When John took it, Joe gripped it tightly and gave it a good hard shake.

"Glad to meet ya'. Any friend of Blondie's and all that." Then he looked down the bar. "Not much room in front, there's a booth free and some of the tables. You'll have to come to the bar and pick up your own drinks; too busy for table service, I'm here alone for now."

"That's fine Joe. I'll have a red wine and…" she turned to John, "you staying with beer, or do you want something else?"

"Draft is fine with me."
"OK Joe, a red wine and a draft beer, a schooner, you know, one of the big ones."

"You got it dearie." He grabbed a bottle from the back bar and went to the beer taps. When he returned he had a glass of wine and a large heavy stemmed glass of beer. When John pulled out his wallet, Joe waved him off.

"I'll run a tab, too busy to be screwin' around making change."

"Thanks Joe," Carol said smiling, then she set the Styrofoam container with her leftover dinner in it on the bar. "Could you stick this somewhere cold for me? Call it collateral."

"Anything honey," he picked it up, "it'll be in with the imported bottle beer."

They retreated behind the partition and sat down at a table, one of four. There was one other couple at the last table. It was actually quite private, especially compared to the scene at the bar.

"So," she looked at him, "what do we talk about?"

"Anything, everything, whatever; mostly I'd like to hear about you."

"Not much to tell."

Well, still have dreams of being an actress?"

"No, that died a long time ago."

"And you stayed on in New York. I don't even know where you were from originally."

"Steubenville, Ohio, and you?"

"Rochester, we're from roughly the same part of the world. We both came to the city to make it big, and we both came up short. How about that?"

She was leaning over the table, staring down at

her wine glass. When she raised her head up and looked at him, it seemed to John as if all the sadness in the world was written on her face.

"The similarity ends about there, though." She tipped her head slightly, shaking it. "Are you sure you want to hear this?"

"Only if you want to tell it; I don't want to…" he paused, trying to express himself, "if you don't want to, don't. I don't want to upset you."

"No, it's all right. Perhaps you should know. You'll probably find out sooner or later." She placed her elbow on the table, rested her chin in the palm of her hand and looked at him. "I started dating this guy, another aspiring thespian, and I got pregnant. So, we got married; lasted about two years. He used to get an allowance from home. What I didn't know was his family had money, lots of it. They never acknowledged me or the marriage. They thought I was some cheap little gold digger after the family fortune. The thing was, I didn't even know there was a family fortune."

"The whole thing was a God damned joke and the joke was on me." Her voice had taken on a bitter edge. "I thought we were in love, but I was wrong. Once we were married his true nature came out. He blamed me for getting pregnant, like he had nothing to do with it. He followed his family's belief that I'd set out to trap him, to ruin his life. He became abusive. After a couple of years, he got tired of slapping me around, so we got divorced. His family was thrilled, they gave me what I thought was a nice little settlement. He got custody of our daughter. I was supposed to have unlimited visitation rights. That seemed fair; I hated to lose the child, but as I said, he had money and I didn't even have a job. The practical side of me said it was better that way no matter how heart breaking it was for me."

"The problem was, the settlement wasn't really all that big, when you're poor, it sounded like a lot of money. There's a moment when it hits you that that's all you have, that it's not enough to live on for any length of time. So I took a job in one of those places where they rented out cameras and models to people who claimed to be amateur photographers so they could take picture of you, usually in the nude. There were a lot of those places around back then. Some of the customers seemed to actually be amateur photographers; they were getting their jollies looking at naked girls, but they had you posing somewhat artistically. But most, they wanted you in some pretty strange and humiliating positions." She glanced over her shoulder to see if anyone was within earshot. "They wanted you to finger yourself, masturbate, you know, that sort of thing."

"Once my ex got himself and our daughter back home in Carolina, his family lawyers went to work. They found out about what I was doing and one day I got a legal document served to me stating that I was morally unfit to be a mother, that I was not to have any visitation rights beyond what he agreed to and he wasn't agreeing to any. I don't know if it would have stood up in New York State, but the child was down there with him. I couldn't afford a lawyer so I gave it up as a lost cause. I didn't see where I could do anything."

Watching her, John could see reliving all this in her mind was affecting her. She had become tense and appeared uncomfortable. Remembering Rita's warning about Carol having been damaged, he wished there was a way to stop this, but it was like he'd broken a milk carton; there was nothing left to do but let it drain and hope there was a way to clean up the mess. He also thought she had been right, the similarities in their stories had ended quickly. After his brief attempt at writing had failed, he had a degree to fall back on. Carol had only her wits, and sometimes that's not enough. He wanted to ask about the daughter, but felt it might add to her pain; now was not the time.

"Another drink?" he asked quietly.

"Yes, please."

He took their empty glasses and headed for the bar. He was hoping the time it took getting them would give her a respite, a chance to either relax or change the topic entirely. Out at the bar, Joe looked over and saw him.

"Ready for another?"

John nodded and set the two glasses down. He watched as Joe grabbed a couple of fresh ones and filled them. When he brought them over, he managed a smile on his unfriendly face.

"How're you and Blondie doin' back there, alright?"

"Oh, fine, having a good time."

"Good, enjoy," he grabbed the empty glasses and started to walk away, then he paused. "She's a special girl, you're lucky."

John picked up the drinks and returned to the table. He couldn't help but think no matter how bad her past had been, she seemed to be blessed with some good friends now. He also wondered if she knew this. When he placed her wine in front of her she gave him a bland smile and thank you, the type one gives a waiter or waitress. He wasn't insulted by it, merely curious.

"Joe was asking how we were doing."

"Did you tell him I was boring the hell out of you?"

"No, why in God's name would I say that?"

"Because people don't like hearing about other

people's problems, sob stories don't interest them."

There was no anger or reproach in her voice, in fact it was pleasant and matter of fact sounding. John, however, was confused by what he saw as a mood change. He thought to himself momentarily before saying anything.

"I really hope you don't think I was prying, but I wasn't bored. I just wanted to learn about you. You know, as a friend. I don't want you to tell me about anything that makes you uncomfortable, if that's the problem. I wanted to get to know you, that's all."

"No...no, it's nothing like that," she looked at him with the little one sided smile she often had. "I really don't want to be that person that unloads all their problems on everyone. I don't want people feeling sorry for me or thinking I'm looking for sympathy. If you really want to know, I'm willing to tell."

"It's all up to you."

"OK," she nodded her head, "you asked for it. Losing my daughter was the worst thing that could have happened to me. Unless something like that has happened to you, you can't imagine how awful it is. It would have been easier if she had died, but to know she was alive somewhere and you weren't allowed any contact, you didn't even know if she knew you were alive, to be told you weren't fit to be near your own flesh and blood…"

She closed her eyes and shook her head. John slid his hand across the table and placed it on top of hers. It was a feeble attempt to comfort her, but it was the best he could muster.

"I went sort of off the deep end after that. I became basically a party girl. Heavy into weed and coke, a line of blow killed the pain every time. There's a spiral there, you use to feel good, then afterwards you feel shitty, so you use some more to get feeling righteous again. In that condition, there aren't a lot of job opportunities around. I started working in the strip joints and the peep shows uptown. The peep shows were the worst, you know, the ones where guys dropped a token in the box and the curtain opened, there one of us would be behind the glass. We'd do whatever foolishness, they'd like. It made the camera places look tame. Squirming and wiggling in fake ecstasy while some slug jerks off doesn't do a lot for your self-esteem. But, that's what we were supposed to do. They only got a few minutes before the curtain closed, so you wanted to get them hot and bothered so they'd spend more to watch while they got themselves off."

She looked at his hand covering hers as if she hadn't been aware of it until then. Reaching over with her free hand, she patted the back of his lightly in acknowledgment. She looked at him, again with the sad smile that belongs to the long suffering ones. Seeing that look on her face, he moved his hand slightly and gripped hers gently.

"The thing is, drugs and the sex trade go hand in hand. Some take the jobs to pay for their habit, other come to it clean, then use the drugs to make themselves feel better about it. It doesn't matter which came first, drugs were readily available, it's like the people in the suits with their martini laced lunches. It's a part of the life style."

Carol removed her hand from under his and lifted her glass, holding it two handed. John realized she was trying to hide a nervous tremor. She took a sip, set the glass down, crossed her arms, and leaned forward on her elbows.

"You don't think things out clearly when you're constantly under the influence. This clown I was living with talked me into getting a breast enlargement; silicone. 'Bigger tits means bigger tips' he said. That made sense to me, so I had it done. They were impressive at first," she leaned back and held her hands in front of her chest, several inches in front of her breasts.

"Unfortunately, it was a bad job. After two years the implants began to leak, there was an infection and I had to have them removed. Then there was a need for reconstructive surgery to get my breasts back to looking normal."

"All this was expensive. Strippers don't have health insurance, and the asshole who talked me into it in the first place was long gone. Before he left though, he broke my jaw and took out a bunch of my teeth with a whiskey bottle."

John winced when he heard that. It explained the one sided smile. He began to wonder if there had been any happiness in this girl's life. As he thought, his eyes drifted down to her chest. Seeing this, Carol lowered her head, looking at her breasts. Then she tipped her head slightly and looked at him.

"They look normal, there is some light scarring. Other than that, there's nothing unusual about them."

"I'm sorry," he was embarrassed now, "I didn't mean anything, I didn't mean to stare."

"It's OK, in the business I'm in I get worried if guys don't look. Besides, I understand that it's a natural reaction. I brought the subject up so I can't get too mad if you're curious."

"I just don't want to insult you or piss you off." Now it was her turn to reassure him, this time it was her hand that covered his. She flashed him the good smile, the one that lit up her whole face. He had the feeling she was comfortable around him and it made him happy. The conversation lightened up after that, there was no more talk of troubles or hardship, they were merely a middle aged couple enjoying each other's company. After they left the bar, walking back to her building, she felt the need to explain something.

"Look, I want you to know one thing. Through all that went on in my life back then, I never turned myself out. I never went to the streets, you know, whoring. A lot of what I did might be considered that, all the sleeping around and that, but there's a difference. I want you to know that."

"Hey, you did what you thought you had to do to get by, who am I to judge?"

"Well, I really want you to know I don't do that sort of thing anymore."

"So, you're telling me, nothing's going to happen tonight?" He had made every effort to make sure she knew he was joking. In the light of the store fronts he saw she was looking at him and smiling. She suddenly sidestepped shouldering into him, the same movement she made on the way to the bar.

"Not tonight anyway. But, keep trying there, Romeo, it could happen someday." The mood had shifted from serious to playful.

In front of her apartment door it turned serious again. He went to kiss her good night, a simple kiss, but couldn't control himself. He basically swept her up, embraced her tightly and kissed her full on the lips, hard and passionately. She, in turn, pressed herself against him, arms around his neck, receiving the kiss with matching ardor. When their lips parted, they both stepped back from each other, Carol leaning against the door.

"Would you like to come in for a while?"

He wanted to desperately, but he remembered her backstory. This was a woman who'd been used and abused. The last thing she needed was to feel like he was trying to take advantage of her. On the other hand, he didn't want her to think he was rejecting her. He placed his hands on her shoulders.

"No, I'd really like to, but I've got to get up early tomorrow. Real life has a way of interfering with what we want; unfortunately, this is one of those times."

"And am I going to see you again?"

"Count on it, in fact I was thinking about Wednesday night, if you're free."

"Working Wednesday."

"Oh, I thought you only worked days."

"No, not dancing, I have a part time job in a second hand shop in the neighborhood. I told them I would work and I don't want to cancel out on them."

"Saturday then, about the same time?"

"Saturday works for me, I'll be waiting."

"Good, I'll call you later in the week to work out the details. Think of where we can go or what we can do."

His last statement bothered him, he was afraid it sounded like he just wanted to be entertained. He really just wanted to spend time with her. He slid his right hand from her shoulder up her neck to the side of her face.

"I'll be counting the days until then," he said, then leaned forward and kissed her, softly and gently.

He stepped back, turned and began walking away. He hoped desperately that he hadn't misplayed his hand as he headed for the stairs.

"John," hearing her voice he turned and looked back at her. "I really did enjoy myself tonight, thanks."

3:REVELATION

Saturday was too far away for John. Wednesday night he drove downtown to Carol's neighborhood, got out and began walking, looking at the store fronts. He was searching for second hand shops, for the second hand shop to be exact. He could have called and asked either Rita or Carol herself where it was, but for some reason he wanted to find it himself.

His task was complicated by the simple fact he wasn't too sure just what she meant by second hand shop. He passed several pawn shops, costume shops, and just plain junk stores that could have qualified. Finally looking in the window of one he caught a glimpse of the blonde hair pulled back in a ponytail. He knew he'd found the right place.

Opening the door, he went in and looked around. It seemed to be an eclectic assortment of used merchandise; reusable clothing, old hand tools, serviceable housewares, etc. But, mostly he was looking at the blonde ponytail with the darker streaks running through it. She turned her head looking over her shoulder to see who'd come in. Recognition was almost instantaneous; she broke into a wide smile.

"John, what are you doing here?"

"I was looking for some, ah, new spats and this looked like the place to find them. White ones to go with my brown Florsheims, the old ones are really looking ratty. Got any in stock there, my good woman?"

"Afraid not, wrong store, wrong century, we're all out of spats. We sold the last pair we had sixty years ago, to Fred Astaire, I believe."

"Ah, damn my luck. Well, Fred probably needed them more than me."

She walked over and leaned back against a table full of kitchenware, her arms folded across her chest. Her lips were pressed tightly together in an obvious attempt to suppress a smile. Tonight there was none of the sadness on her face that he'd seem on Saturday. It did him good to realize she was glad to see him.

"So, why are you really here? On a scavenger hunt or something?"

"Like you don't know," he grinned at her, "I wanted to see you. I thought this would be better than a phone call. Did I do wrong?"

She turned her head to the side, smiling broadly now with a kind of silent laugh. When she turned back, still smiling, John was amazed at how her inner beauty showed on her face. She actually looked years younger. He was even more amazed that he could be the cause of such a transformation. He had a giddy feeling deep inside.

"Whatever the reason, I'm glad you came. I'm glad to see you."

"Are we still on for Saturday?" She nodded her head eagerly. "Good, any ideas where we could go?"

"Sort of," she said, "a movie works, but I was wondering, do you like to dance, like slow dancing, that sort of thing? I know a place."
He shrugged his shoulders. In reality, he never was much of a dancer, but he wanted to do something she enjoyed.

"Funny you should have mentioned Fred Astaire, because I ain't him. So, if you're willing to put up with my awkward leads and getting your toes mashed occasionally, I'm game."

"No, I don't want to force you into doing something you don't like."

"Are you saying you won't work with me? Because now I've suddenly got this great desire to improve my slow dancing skills. Do you really want to deny me that?"

"OK, if you put it that way, that's we're headed. Just tell me, how bad are you? Do I have to go out and get a pair of steel toed pumps to wear?"

"Well, I don't know if you have to go looking for some, but if there's a pair in here in the clothing section, it might pay you to grab them, just in case."

"All I can say," she said, shaking her head, "is this could be interesting."

Saturday night, they went to a small Italian restaurant that Carol knew. She insisted that they go somewhere less expensive. It was actually a good idea, spaghetti and meatballs washed down with a sound Chianti costing less than one of last week's steaks. It was a very satisfying meal. Of course, John probably would have enjoyed a Spam sandwich if he was eating it with Carol.

From there she led the way to a bar several blocks away. From the outside it looked like any other bar, but once inside, behind the narrow barroom, he could see the back room. Expanding into the neighboring establishment, it was much wider than the bar area. In the dim light he could see couples dancing. He'd been expecting a much bigger place, not that he minded, as long as he was with her.

"Get us a couple of drinks, wine for me," she said, "I'll head back and grab us a table."

Ordering the drinks, he made his way into the backroom with them, then he stopped and looked around for her. The center of the room was open for dancing, chairs and small tables were scattered around the perimeter. In some places two or three tables had been pushed together to accommodate larger groups. When he spotted the two arms waving back and forth trying to get his attention, he headed in her direction.

He sat down and placed her wine in front of her. He took the glass that had been placed upside down over the neck of his beer bottle off and pushed it aside, deciding he'd rather drink from the bottle. He hoped she wouldn't think he was being crude, but it seemed stupid to him to bother with such a small glass. He needn't have worried; she never noticed one way or another.

"Do you come here often?"

"No," she replied, "hardly ever, but sometimes Rita and I do drop in, hoping to meet somebody, but that never happens."

"Really? I would have thought guys would be all over you two."

"No, I mean there's a lot of horny guys in the bar that come looking for an easy mark, a quick jump, but you get enough of those people when you work at a strip club. I don't think I've ever met anybody nice here, someone you wanted to get to know better. Don't get me wrong, there are a lot of nice guys here, but they usually come with someone."

"I can see your point." He raised his bottle and took a drink, then second guessed himself; he felt like a slob. Taking the glass and, tipping it slightly, filled it. Manners had won out.

"I'm a little disappointed," she remarked, "on the weekends, they often have live music. Nothing fancy, usually a quartet or a piano player, but tonight we have to listen to canned music."

"I don't see that as a problem, I came here to be with you, not some string quartet."

"You silver tongued devil," she leaned forward on the table, "where the hell have you been all my life, and more importantly, why hasn't somebody grabbed you up for her own?"

"Someone did; grabbed me up, chewed me up, then spit me out. It wasn't a pleasant experience."

"Her loss. But, let's find out if you're as bad a dancer as you've been saying."

He was glad she didn't press him farther about his ex-wife. He didn't like talking about it. It was funny, she didn't have any trouble talking about the tragedy that had been her earlier life, but he didn't want to tell about his one real failing. It wasn't lost on him and he was somewhat embarrassed by that fact as she led him out onto the floor.

It was apparent to him that she was expecting the worst in the first dance. Fortunately he didn't deliver it but did an adequate job. His biggest problem was a lack of confidence, he was unsure of himself. Still he led her gracefully, managed to not step on her toes or cross her up. At one point she looked up at him.

"You're not doing so badly."

"Not doing real good either."

"Nonsense, you just need practice."
They returned to their table at the end of the song and quietly sipped their drinks.

"Do you mind if I ask you something?" Her voice was low.

"No, go ahead, anything."

"You mentioned your ex-wife, what happened there?"

"Nothing really, maybe everything, I'm not all that sure. Bottom line is, I married her because she was good looking, she married me because she thought I had some kind of a big future. We were pretty much a mismatch. She tried turning me into something I wasn't. I didn't like that and rebelled. We fought a lot, then got divorced; end of story. The big problem is, it left me leery of getting too deeply involved with anyone again."

After he finished, he realized that telling a woman he was interested in and cared for that he was afraid of committing himself to a long term relationship wasn't the wisest move he could have made. And the problems of his marriage were petty compared to what she'd endured.

"It sounds silly, I know. But, that's the way it was. After the divorce I kind of crawled into my shell."

"I don't think it's silly. No one should try and force you to be something you don't want to be. What was it she wanted to turn you into anyway?"

"God damned if I know. I'm a school teacher, nothing more, nothing less. Granted the type of school I work at pays better than I'd get in the public sector, but I'm still a teacher, period. Never claimed to be anything else"

They sat out a couple of songs before taking the floor again. That was the pattern for the night; getting up to dance every third or fourth song, sitting back and watching the others in between. John would get up and go to the bar to refresh their drinks as needed.

Finally as they danced to an instrumental version of "Smoke Gets in Your Eyes" he kissed her on the cheek. Surprised, she looked up at him and he kissed her lightly on the lips. She broke into

a smile and laid her head on his shoulder. He felt
her arm around his waist tighten as she pulled
herself closer to him. He rested his cheek in her hair
as she moved her hand from his and draped it over
his other shoulder. They clung to each other,
looking like two hormonally driven teen agers at a
high school dance, rocking back and forth slowly to
the rhythm of the music. They weren't dancing so
much as making love, both wishing the song would
never end.

The song did end, and they returned to their
table, both knowing something had happened. There
was no longer any doubt in their minds about
whether they liked each other, now it was a given.
The question now was how far did they want it to
go. Both had been burned in the past by false loves
and neither wanted it to happen again. But the
difference was apparent, there was no more feeling
each other out emotionally, now they talked as if
they were old friends rather than two people who
had only met two weeks earlier. They were
completely comfortable together.

He walked her home that night hand in hand.
There could be no doubt in the minds of any who
saw them that they were a couple. At her door the
scene was similar to the one last week, a passion
filled good night kiss that left them both breathless
and somewhat frustrated. John had decided to
himself that he wasn't going to try to take this to the
next level until he felt it was right. Carol herself
wanted to wait; to be sure he wasn't just looking for

a quick lay. It wouldn't have bothered her that much if he did, but she wanted to find out, to know for sure.

Within a week, they no longer had to ask if the other was available on any given night, they knew each other's schedule. The question was no longer "do you want to go somewhere" but "what do you want to do tonight". They were spending more and more time together, becoming closer, but still neither made any move towards the bedroom. They were like two adolescents, sex was on both their minds, but both seemed to be afraid to mention it. Neither wanted the other to think that's all they were after.

It was during this period, as they grew more at ease with each other, that Carol began to talk more openly about her past. Mostly it was about specific incidents, conversations, and the like, but slowly she began to open up about how far she had sunk during that period. Some of it came as a surprise to him. Perhaps shocking would be a better word. It was after dinner one night that she made one of those revelations.

It had been a pleasant meal, he'd made a cold pasta salad and it had gone well on a hot humid night in the city. After they'd finished eating, Carol leaned over the table on her elbow. Her chin rested in the palm of her hand while she looked down at her plate. Her other hand pushed the handle of her fork back and forth where it stuck out over the edge of the dish. She seemed lost in thought.

"Look, there are some things you should know about me"

"Such as?" He thought he'd already heard all there was to hear.

"When I went through my bad years, I posed for a lot of nude photos."

"Well, yeah, you told me that. At those photo places, right?"

"No, I mean professionally. You'd pose for a real photographer, get paid, and the pictures belonged to him. He would, I guess you'd call it broker them out to things like the cheap skin magazines and these pulp sex newspaper things.

They were the worst. Open them up, and there'd be a big headline, 'MOM SEXES HER THREE SONS' above a pornographic incest story with my picture, naked as the day I was born next to it. It looked like I was the one who was screwing her kids."

"Not so bad, I wouldn't mind seeing then actually."

"You'd be able to see me in my brief big breasted days, and after I had the implants removed. You could make comparisons."

"I like the way you look now."

"Sweet, but the thing is, those pictures are out there and they can turn up any time. I thought you should know that."

"OK, now I know. It's not that big of a deal. In fact, in view of what you've told me before, it's not that big of a surprise."

"No? Trouble is, there's more. I've posed for pornography too. Still photos and I did a few loops."

"Loops?"

"Loops are those short films they show in peep shows, the ones where you drop a quarter in and see a part of it, then wind up spending about two bucks to see the whole thing. The stills, some went to hard core magazines, others were sold through the mail. They're still out there also."

This was an actual shock. He couldn't imagine the woman sitting in front of him doing such a thing. He tried to keep his expression blank, but Carol saw something in his face.

"You can't tell me you've never looked at that sort of thing."

"No," he admitted sheepishly, "I have seen my

share of porn, maybe more than my share."

"Did you ever wonder about the girls that were in it?"

"No, I guess not, not really. I mean, I often wondered what it would be like to be with one of them, but that's about all."

"They're just women, women like me, trying to make a living. Horrified? Want to run away from me or anything like that?"

The fact was that he was shocked and disappointed. Not disappointed in her, but disappointed that she had felt the need to do something like that. Disgusted that fate could have driven her to such extremes. The old cliché "there but for fortune" ran through his head. If it could happen to her it could happen to anyone.

"No, I'm not going anywhere," he assured her. "It's ancient history. You did what you thought you had to do. Who am I to judge you? Like you said, you were trying to make a living"

"I was in Viet Nam," he said after a brief pause, "I killed a couple of people, you know the other guys. I was doing what I had to do. So, we both did what we had to do. You had sex with someone and I killed some poor North Vietnamese bastards. So, you tell me who has the darker past? Which act was the most immoral? I personally don't see either of us as having done anything wrong."

He figured it was time to move on, to change the subject, and hopefully set her mind at ease. A thought had been floating in his mind for a few days, and now seemed to be the right time to bring it up.

"When's the last time you went on vacation?"

"Vacation?" She sounded confused. "I don't know, I've been to the Jersey shore a few times, but not in a while, why?"

"I was planning on running up to Saratoga to take in a concert. Highbrow stuff, philharmonic music, I don't know if you're interested in that type of thing or not, but if you are, would you like to come with?"

"When would you be going?"

"Friday of next week, come back on Sunday. It's on me, think you can get away?"

"Probably, I've never been up there, what's it like?"

"Beautiful, restful, the Arts Center is in a state park, surrounded by trees and manicured lawns. The old mineral springs are scattered around in the parks and in some cases on the streets. It's something to see. You coming?"

"Sounds lovely, all I'd ever heard about it was the horse races. I'd like to see it. Count me in, if you really don't mind."

How could he mind?

The ride up to Saratoga Springs was interesting. Carol had never been farther north of the city than New Rochelle so her views of New York State were something new and exciting to her. Slowly a different word was unfolding in before her. Even from the interstate, the Hudson valley impressed her; somehow she'd envisioned this part of "up state" as an endless string of suburbs. She was impressed with the long stretches of forests, orchards and farmlands. John was pleased she'd agreed to come, happy that she was enjoying the ride, but mostly grateful to be with her.

Saratoga Springs in the summer is a vibrant, busy place. Crowded, with heavy traffic, it is filled with a mix of all types of people; the rich with their summer homes, people coming to the concerts at the Performing Arts Center, tourists stopping by to "take the waters", history buffs wanting to see the old Revolutionary War battlefield, and horse race aficionados. It's a multi-faceted venue ranging from nearby lakes in rural settings to the center of town where the wide thoroughfare known, appropriately, as Broadway has a decidedly big city, urban feel to it. One thing John knew, there would be something here Carol would enjoy, no matter what she preferred.

They checked into their motel, and hauled their bags up to the room. It was a typical chain motel room, just like millions across the country; bright and airy but antiseptically bland. But Carol seemed pleased; she had lived the last two decades of her life in inexpensive cluttered apartments, so to her the room seemed luxurious.

"I don't know about you, but I'm hungry," he told her after they were all settled in. "Why don't we take a walk up the street and get a bite, unless you'd rather do something else."

"Now that you mention it," she responded, "I could eat. Know anywhere good?"

"No, this place is like any other resort, it's constantly changing. Every time you come here half the restaurants are different. I haven't been here in a few years, so we'll have to go exploring."

They went out and walked up Broadway, doing all the typical tourist things. He took her into Congress Park, leading her over to one of Saratoga's famous springs. She cupped one hand to catch a sample and tasted it. She reacted as most uninitiated people do; she made a face and spat it out.

"Good Gawd! Do people really drink this shit?"

"Oh yeah, locals have been known to fill up jugs to take home with them."

He cupped both hands together and let them fill with water. He drank the double handful down.

"It's not so bad, plus it keeps you regular."

"I think I'll risk constipation, thank you."
From there they went up the street, pausing to look at the menus posted in window fronts.

"I was thinking about something small, and then we could have a good meal this evening before going to the concert. Then again, we could eat heavy now and have something light later on. What do you think?"

"I think it's too hot to have anything heavy now" she said, "maybe we should wait until tonight for the big meal."

They decided on a place that had a large selection of cold salads on the luncheon menu. There were some tables outside, but the thought of sitting in the hot sun convinced them to eat inside. They did manage to get a table close to the window where they could watch the passing parade of people on the sidewalk as they ate their meal.

"This does seem nice up here," Carol observed between bites of her chicken salad, "I can see why you like it. Is it like this where you live? I don't want to sound stupid, but I've never really seen much of New York State, just the city."

"You don't sound stupid. Mackenzie Academy is in the Finger Lakes region, it's much more sedate than here, but it has its own beauty."

"You'll have to show me it sometime."

"Any time you want, you've got a standing invitation. For that matter, you're welcome to go with me anywhere else I go."

He studied her face for a reaction. He wasn't too sure if she realized what he'd said, she didn't show any immediate response. When she finally responded, it wasn't what he'd been hoping to hear.

"Well, we'll have to see about that when the time comes."

He wasn't sure what he'd expected, but that wasn't it. He'd hoped for her to be a little more enthusiastic, but it never occurred to him that she might be as unsure of herself as he was. He didn't answer, refusing to give away his feelings; he finished his pasta and bean salad. When they left the restaurant, they walked up and down the street stopping at souvenir and gift shops. Carol bought a couple of sweatshirts, one for herself and one to take back for Rita. After that they went back to the motel. John had suggested going out to the pool for a swim. It was a hot, sunny afternoon and a dip in the water seemed like the thing to do.

When he'd first mentioned to her back in the city to bring a bathing suit, she'd confessed she hadn't been swimming in years and didn't even own a suit. She'd picked out a used one at the second hand shop and brought that. She went into the bathroom to change while he put his trunks on in the room. He couldn't help but wonder why a woman who danced in a strip club, who'd been involved with pornography, was so shy about undressing in front of him. When she came out she was wearing a dark blue one piece suit.

"Do I look alright?"

"Of course, what makes you think otherwise?"

"I guess I'm just uncomfortable in this suit."

"Nonsense, you look great."

He still couldn't understand. He would have thought a woman with her past and present wouldn't be the least bit reluctant to go out in public in a bathing suit, and a one piece at that. It never occurred to him that someone who had been exploited to the degree she had may have developed major self-esteem issues around "polite society". There was a difference between working naked at a peep show and walking down the hallway to the pool in a hotel wearing a bathing suit; that difference made her self-conscious.

Out at the pool, John spent most of the time in the water while Carol preferred to sit poolside in the sun and watch. She'd taken an initial dip in, trying unsuccessfully to keep her hair dry, before retreating to a lounge chair. At one point she left to go to the room to get money for the soda machine, returning with a can of ginger ale. John got out of the water and sat on the chair next to hers.

"You're not bored are you?"

"Oh, no," she shook her head, pony tail swinging side to side, "I'm happy sitting here in the sun. Do you realize how seldom I get to do this in the city? Never, keep swimming if you want, I'm fine here, I enjoy it."

"You're sure you don't mind? I feel like I'm ignoring you here."

"Don't be silly," she gestured towards the water with her hand, "go, enjoy yourself."

He returned to the water. For somebody who loves to swim, it's difficult to understand why others don't. He was mystified by the fact that she didn't want to come into the pool on so hot a day. But then again, the pool was amazingly empty, he was one of a small handful in the water. Perhaps there were more people that felt like her than like him.

He continued to lazily swim laps up and down the length of the pool, then he noticed her get up and walk over to the edge of the pool, leaving her sun glasses and soda behind. She sat down and let her feet and legs dangle in the water. He swam over, placing his forearms on either side of her slender thighs, looking up at her.

"Just dropping by for a visit?" he asked.

"Something like that, you were worried about ignoring me, now it's my turn to worry about ignoring you."

"Absolutely nothing to worry about, as long as you're happy, I'm happy."

Wordlessly, smiling her one sided smile, Carol raised her leg, bending at the knee. She placed her foot against his chest and pushed him backwards, then slid into the pool.

"OK, I guess I'll join you."

With that she dipped herself under the water and came up swimming towards the deep end. She was a weak swimmer, John caught up with her easily. At the end of the pool, she tossed an arm over the edge, holding on while he treaded water.

"I've been watching you; you really love the water, don't you?"

"Oh yeah," he laughed, "part fish."

"Well, you just seem to be a natural, like you're completely at home in the deep end."

"I'm at home in either end."

He began to slowly backstroke his way towards the shallow end, looking back at her. Carol pushed off from the wall of the pool following him. He kept his speed down so she could keep up. Reaching the shallow end, he sat down. Carol caught up and sat beside him. Her wet hair was clinging to her head, bangs all askew.

"I hope there'll be time for me to do my hair."

"Of course, the show doesn't start until twenty after eight. You'll have plenty of time. Besides, if you went looking like you do now, it'd be all right. You look good to me."

"Yeah," she looked down into the water trying to suppress a grin, "if you like the drowned rat look."

"So, maybe I like blonde rats."
She giggled, scooped up a handful of water and threw it in his face. He laughed as he shook the it off.

"About tonight, the tickets I have are for seats, but the weather is supposed to be great tonight, I thought maybe we could sit on the lawn and see the show from there."

"Is that good? Remember, I've never been there."

"The Art Center an open air venue, it's built at the bottom of a hillside. When you sit on the lawn, you're still looking down at the stage, you're just farther away. For acts like this, they don't care if you bring in food and some, uh, libations. I've got a bottle of wine icing down in the waste basket in the room. I figured we take that, stop somewhere and get some cheese and crackers and have ourselves a little picnic. There's a blanket in my car. What do you think?"

"Seems like a good idea to me. You're the expert here, let's do it your way."

4:SEDUCTION

They walked around the grounds of the Art Center that evening, following the crowd, looking at the vendor's stands. He bought Carol a souvenir T-shirt despite her protesting that she didn't need one. He ignored her, insisting it was a touristy thing to do. Finally, they went down and selected a place on the hillside and spread their blanket. John set down the insulated bag holding the bottle of wine and the cheese they'd picked up on the way over.

"I can see what you meant," she looked at the unobstructed view down to the stage, "it'll sort of be like a picnic with live music."

"That was the idea, but like I said, we have seats, if you'd rather sit under the roof."

"No, do you know how long it's been since I was on a picnic? I say we stay here."

She sat down, leaning forward on her drawn up knees. She looked up at him smiling and batted her eyes theatrically.

"Care to join me there, sailor?"

"Gosh ma'am," he replied in a fake hayseed accent, "is all the wimmin' in this town this friendly?"

"Only around good looking sailor boys like you, who just got paid. You did just get paid didn't you?"

"Yes ma'am, only I set my money down on a blanket on the ship to count it and some feller yelled "CRAPS!' and snatched it all up. Durndest thing ever I did see."

"Snatched all your money? Well then, that's the only snatch you'll be seeing tonight." Then she suddenly made a shocked face, realizing what she'd said, and quickly looked around to see if anyone had heard her. "Good God, did I say that? Sorry, I got carried away. I forgot where I was at."

"That's all right," he sat down alongside her, putting his hand on her back reassuringly, "plenty of New York City girls up here, everyone's used to you guys and your filthy mouths."

"Good, there's safety in numbers, I always say. Besides, you're the one who brought the word into the conversation."

"Guilty as charged," he admitted, "I'm just no damned good, a bad influence."

"I know," she said happily, "my parents warned me about people like you when I was a kid."

They waited patiently, watching the crowd as they came in, some heading down to their seats, others staking out a spot on the grass. Below on the stage, they could see the stagehands making their final adjustments to the orchestra's chairs, testing the sound equipment and lighting. Finally they could see the musicians coming in, taking their seats. There was a last minute rush of people who'd been standing around on the upper edge of the amphitheater going down to find their seats. Then there came the confusion of sound as instruments were tested by individuals and sections. The amphitheater lights dimmed as the concert began.

The selection of music was a mix of popular tunes that ranged from depression-era big band sounds through 1970's pop; Glen Miller to Billy Joel. As evening faded into dusk, John fished out the bottle of wine and a cork screw from the bag. Opening it, he handed Carol a plastic cup and filled it.

"Oh, I see we're using the good crystal tonight."

"Yes, nothing but the best for you, m'lady." As they sipped their wine, listening to the music, she moved closer and leaned against him. He put his arm around her, he could hear her humming softly to herself along with the song, felt her body swaying slightly almost undetectably with the music. It seemed to him that he'd never wanted to be with another woman as badly as he wanted to be with her now. He wanted to tell her this, but wasn't sure how or what to say. He didn't want to do or say anything to ruin the moment.

Darkness descended rapidly, contributing to the mood. At one point he noticed her staring up at the sky. Glancing upwards himself, he asked her quietly.

"Something going on up there?"

"No, just looking at the stars. I haven't done that in a long time, so long that I can't remember the last time. You don't notice them in the city too much, but it's hard to ignore them here."

She lowered herself back slowly, lying on her back, one arm behind her head, holding the plastic cup of wine on her stomach. John leaned back on his elbow, looking at her.

"Do you know much about the stars? You know, like their names and the constellations and that type of stuff."

"No, nothing, I just wonder why I've never noticed how beautiful the night sky can be. Look at them all, damn, and I never paid any attention."

"Well, like you said, there's not much opportunity to see it in the city."

"Yeah, but before that I lived in Ohio, didn't notice it back then either." She looked over at him, "Maybe it's the company I'm with."

"You never know." What he didn't mention
was that she'd never know how much he wished it
was the company, how much he wanted to believe
he could be source of the serenity that seemed to
have engulfed her. Silently, he sat up again. He
fished into the bag and brought out two plastic
containers of cubed cheese, then a box of crackers.
Seeing him get the food, Carol sat up.

"Weren't planning on eating alone, were you?"

"A man can always dream, but as long as
you're up," he pointed to first one tub then the
other, "muenster and gouda. You'll have to use your
fingers, didn't bring the silverware."

Sitting on the lawn, sipping wine, nibbling on
cheese and crackers in the darkness, John felt an
incredible sense of closeness to the woman at his
side. The orchestra began playing "Moonlight
Serenade"; it was the perfect setting for a seduction.
If they weren't surrounded by other couples on the
lawn, John would have been tempted to make love
to her then and there. He was bewildered by her
ability to make him feel young again by her mere
presence.

He remembered the feeling he'd had on the
dance floor that night in the city. He had the same
feeling now, one of being a teenager again. That
night, he'd felt like a kid at the high school dance.
Now he felt like he was back at a drive-in movie
with some sweet young thing at his side, trying to

decide whether he should make a move on her, unsure of what that move should be, terrified of doing the wrong thing.

"Carol, are you enjoying yourself?" She turned and looked at him before answering.

"Oh, yeah, God yes, how can you ask that? I can't remember the last time I did anything so... normal, so clean." She leaned over and kissed his cheek, "thanks for bringing me."

On an impulse, he leaned over and kissed her on the lips. It was a brief and simple kiss, but it conveyed an exchange of acceptance between them. It was the beginning of a new phase of their relationship, a sea change that perhaps neither was really ready for.

Finally the orchestra played "Good Night My Love", softly and sweetly, an apparent signal that the concert was coming to an end. Some of the audience began to leave in order to beat the rush. John and Carol stayed put through to the last notes, not moving until the stage lights came on, illuminating the auditorium. Then they repacked the bag with their left overs, Carol folded up the blanket and draped it over her arm. They waited for an opportunity to join in the parade leaving the amphitheater and then followed the crowd to the parking lot.

The lot was a bit of a madhouse, everyone

trying to get out at once was causing a small traffic jam by the exits. John and Carol walked to the car, put away the remnants of their picnic and leaned against the trunk, holding hands, waiting for the congestion to clear out.

"So," he asked cautiously, "what did you think, was it worth the trip?"

"It's beautiful up here, I'm glad we came. Even wandering around the motel in a bathing suit was nice, once I got used to the idea."

Once again he couldn't understand why a woman who worked in a strip club would be uncomfortable in a one piece bathing suit. He figured there had to be a reason, but decided to leave well enough alone.

"I was thinking, tomorrow maybe we could take a ride up into the mountains, the Adirondacks are just up the road. Lake Placid is about an hour and a half ride, two at tops. I figure on an early start, two hours up, two hours back, that leaves plenty of time to look around. Unless you'd rather stay around here."

"What's it like up there? The only thing I know about Lake Placid is the Olympics were there."

"The word that comes to my mind is sublime. I may be prejudiced; I used to go skiing up there on occasion."

"Whatever you think we should do is all right with me. I'm the guest, along for the ride."

"Well, I'd hoped you came along for more than just a ride."

"You know what I meant," she mumbled softly.

She was looking down at her feet. In the shadowy light he couldn't see her expression, then she turned her head slightly looking up at him. She had the same shy stifled tight lipped smile he'd seen in the restaurant the first night they'd gone out together. He felt her hand squeeze his tightly. That was answer enough.

Once the parking lot cleared, they got in the car and left. The short ride back to the motel was slightly uneasy. Both knew what was going to happen, but for some reason neither knew how to act, they were like a couple of virgins on their wedding night. When he glanced over at Carol, she was staring at the dashboard apprehensively. He didn't know what to say, he just kept driving. Arriving at the motel, John parked the car and they got out without saying a word. There was an unsettling tension as they walked to the room.

When he slid the key-card into the slot he looked at Carol, her face was expressionless. He'd hoped there would be some clue as to how she felt, a hint of whether anything was going to happen or not. He began to think her remark about "that's the only snatch you're going to see tonight" was more fact than joke.

Entering the room, he set down the bag of leftovers, still not sure how to proceed. It seemed ridiculous to him, they were two middle aged adults, both experienced in these matters and he was acting like it was his first time. However, because of her past, he didn't want her to think he was taking advantage of her and he didn't want to be added to the list of nameless male bodies that had done so.

Carol went over and stood in front of the dresser, facing the mirror. Reaching behind her she undid the clasp on the bow that held her hair back in its familiar ponytail. She raked her fingers back through it, shaking her head to fluff it out and then allowed it to fall naturally to her shoulders. John came up behind her, moved her hair back from one side and kissed her below the ear, then at the base of her neck. She inhaled sharply, making a slight sucking sound. When she exhaled it was almost a sob. She turned to face him slowly, one hand raised feeling behind her the way one does when moving in total darkness.

Facing him, she had a strange look on her face, almost one of curiosity. She reached up with both hands, placing them at the sides of his face, touching at the wrists. Rising on her toes she kissed him lightly on the lips, and then lowered herself.

She stared into his face as if trying to read something there. Then she slid both arms around his neck and pulled him down to kiss him again, this time it was a hard, lusty, desire filled kiss. She pressed herself tightly against him while their tongues caressed each other passionately.

When the kiss ended, she stepped back and glanced over her shoulder at the beds. Carefully, she walked slowly backwards towards them, her elbows at her sides, hands out, palms turned upwards. Her head tipped to one side, her lips slightly parted, she gestured invitingly with her fingers for him to follow. They kissed once more at the edge of one of the beds, then she sat down and took his hands. Lying back, she pulled him down over her.

Their love making was not what he'd expected. He'd thought that, given her background, she might have become jaded or desensitized to it all. The opposite seemed to be true. She responded to his every move, every kiss, every touch, warmly and sensuously. There seemed to be no false passion in her sobbing moans or in her return embraces. His intimate probing touches brought an honest, somewhat demure reaction. Even the brief, awkward interruption when he went to his overnight bag to get a pack of condoms didn't break the mood. During actual intercourse, she seemed to be close to tears, clinging to him tightly.

When they had finished, he could think of no words to say. He was afraid to speak, afraid of

soiling what had seemed to be a pristine act. He
kissed her with all the passion of their earlier kisses,
hoping it would be enough, hoping she would
understand. It was all he could think of to do.
She was also silent, he wasn't sure if that was a
good thing or not. Then she shifted over slightly,
pulling his arm around her, cuddling close against
him. That's the way they fell asleep.

When he woke up, they were still huddled
together. Her head was on his shoulder and one arm
stretched across his chest. One of her legs was
entwined with his. He looked over at the window,
the closed drapes were slightly illuminated; he
figured it was dawn, but not full daylight. He
moved his hand over and lightly stroked her cheek,
then began smoothing out her hair, carefully so as to
not wake her up. Then he spoke softly, more to
himself than to the sleeping form alongside him.

"I love you lady. I'm not sure why, but God
help me, I do."

He looked up at the ceiling, trying to
understand the whole thing. His reverie was
suddenly broken by her voice.

"I heard that." She slowly raised herself up on
one elbow. "I heard what you said."

Then looking down at him, she leaned over and
kissed him. They made love for the second time.
This time was different, there was no uncertainty,

no self-consciousness, their natural instincts took over. It was a more intense, more emotional experience than their earlier encounter. It left them both exhausted and satisfied.

Afterwards, they slept for a few more hours. When they woke up this time, fully awake and rested, they both felt different. They no longer appeared to be a couple, they were a couple. No longer worried about appearing naked in front of each other, they went about their morning ablutions in complete comfort, readying themselves for the day.

They had a breakfast of bagels and cream cheese with coffee at a popular local bagel shop, then got in the car and headed north on the interstate. Gradually the scenery began to change, from the foothills around Saratoga they drove deeper towards the high peaks region. The views grew more and more impressive. When they finally left the interstate they were in the heart of the Adirondacks. The road had more ups and downs that the interstate, some of the downhills were brake warming runs, John had been up here enough to know to not to ride the brakes to avoid overheating them.

At last they reached the final long uphill climb that meant they were close to their destination. From there the road wound its way past the surrounding mountainous terrain. The ski jumps came into view, rising above the trees in the distance. Carol's reaction was about what one would expect from somebody who'd never seen them before.

"What am I looking at?"

"The ski jumps, from the Olympics."

"I didn't realize they were that high."

"Oh, they're high; you'll get a better look in a couple of minutes."

They drove by them, then John turned off the road into a parking lot.

"Time to stretch our legs," he announced. When they got out he purchased tickets for the elevator to the top then they walked up the hill. At the base of one jump, they rode up. Looking down the ramp to the landing zone was an intimidating site.

"Holy crap," she said, "do people really ski down this thing?"

"Yes they do, all the time."

"Now you said you've come up here skiing, you've never..." she gestured towards the hill.

"Oh, hell no, what're you crazy?" He laughed then added, "I guess the question is do you think

I'm that crazy? Good God, this isn't something you do on a whim, I'm not suicidal."

"Remember, I'm still getting to know you. Not suicidal; that's good to know. Meanwhile, I do love this view."

"You ain't seen nothin' yet, my dear." Returning to the car he drove on, approaching the village. Entering the edge of town, he veered off and continued driving, heading to Whiteface Mountain.

"A clear sunny day like this," he explained, "the view will be spectacular. I want to go there first, you can never tell when some clouds will move in."

They drove on past the entrance to the ski area, a few small motels and drive up hamburger stands, finally at an intersection, he turned and headed towards a rustic looking toll house. He paid his admission, listened patiently while the admissions clerk gave the weather report from the top and advised him to use second gear and rely on engine braking on the way down to save his brakes. They continued on their way. The road twisted and turned, snaking it way up to the summit. It leveled and widened at the top into a narrow parking lot. At one end stood an impressive stone building. Carol looked over at it.

"What is that?"

"They call it the Norman Castle; it hides a turnaround for cars, and the second floor has a gift shop and offices for the employees. The good part is farther up." He reached into the backseat and grabbed a windbreaker jacket and the sweatshirt he'd insisted she bring.

"Here, we'll need these. Even on a day like this the wind cools things off up here."

"I see what you mean," she said, pulling on the sweatshirt outside the car. "You say there's more?"

"Yep, this isn't the peak. There's a footpath up, but it's kind of rugged. I think you might like the elevator better."

"There's an elevator?"

"Yeah, it leads to a weather station on the summit."

They walked down a tunnel, waited for the elevator, then rode up. Stepping out of the weather station, they stopped to take it all in

"You weren't kidding, this really is breathtaking." She turned to him, "Do you know what everything is down there?"

"No, Lake Placid is over there and Upper and Lower Saranac are here, and that's about it.

Anything beyond that would be pure guesswork."
"Do you come up here often?"

"Not really, I wouldn't want to do it too often,
it might get boring. Once every four or five years is
good, it keeps it special. I remember one time
though, it'd rained the night before and it was still
pretty cloudy the next morning. I drove over hoping
that it would clear by the time I got here. It hadn't,
but they told me down below it was starting to clear
up top and the fog wasn't bad enough to close the
road, so if I wanted to gamble on it clearing, I could
go ahead. I did, it was kind of creepy driving up in
the fog, but when I got here, the sun was burning it
off. The clouds were below me and the sky up here
was bright and sunny. All these higher peaks were
rising up out of the mist. They looked like islands
rising up out of a wispy white ocean. Man, it really
was something."

"Sounds beautiful, I'm trying to picture it."
She walked over and hopped up on a boulder,
surveying the view. One leg was folded under her,
the other dangling off the rock. It put him in mind
of something. He walked over and stood alongside
her.

"You know, Schlitz beer had an ad campaign
featuring "the girl on the globe" sometimes called
the golden goddess. Right now, in that pose, you
remind me of her. She didn't have a ponytail and
she was wearing some kind of toga, but still, you
put me in mind of her."

"Oh, a goddess now," she laughed, then broke into a very poor phony Southern accent. "Why sur, how you do talk! Best hush now, a girl might get the impression y'all are tryin' to palaver yore way into her pantaloons."

"Frankly Scarlett, I can't think of a nicer place to bullshit my way into."

"OK," her leg swung out lazily hitting him lightly behind his knee, "who's got the dirty mouth today? Not us New York City girls."

"The tables have turned, this time you're the one who brought the subject up. Guess we're both bad influences."

"Good thing we're together," she acknowledged, "that way we can't corrupt the morals of any innocent beings, only each other and we're both pretty well corrupted already."

She slid off the rock and they waked around, admiring the view from all points. When they had their fill and concluded it was time to leave, John pointed out the rocky footpath down to the castle. Carol decided the elevator was a better idea. They made the slow ride down the mountain, then headed back to Lake Placid. Arriving in the village, they headed for a restaurant to get something to eat.

Afterwards, they walked down the street stopping in at all the souvenir shops. They then

continued on, walking around Mirror Lake,
speculating as to just how rich the people were who
owned the lakefront cottages. Strolling hand in
hand, they looked like an attractive middle aged
couple, which is the way they were thinking of
themselves.

From there they headed back to the interstate
and Saratoga. As they came down from the
mountains, they could feel the heat and humidity
retuning. It was a sign that that part of their little
outing was over. They were reminded of the high
temperatures waiting for them in Saratoga, and the
even more oppressive mugginess of Manhattan that
they would have to face the following day. The cool
rarified air of the high peaks was behind them.

When they were back in their motel room,
Carol remarked how nice it was to leave the room a
mess in the morning, then return in the afternoon to
find it neat as a pin. John couldn't help thinking
only one bed was a mess, of course, they had made
a real mess of it.

That evening they went out to eat late, after that
they walked up and down the street, watching the
crowd. On one of the side streets a steady stream of
revelers were coming and going out of a bar. They
went down, thinking of joining in, and having a few
drinks. Looking in at the crowded barroom through
the window, they decided against it. Tired from all
the driving and walking they had done, they decided
they'd rather spend this last night alone with each

other.

Returning to the motel room, they fully intended to make a night of it, but the accumulated fatigue of the last two days had taken its toll on them. They made love once, then literally fell into an exhausted sleep afterwards, not waking up until morning. The television was left playing, unwatched, all night long.

When they woke up in the morning, they were both well rested. There was a certain sadness about them as they readied themselves for the return drive to the city. It was as if neither knew whether their little affair was going to end when they got back or if it was going to continue. For some reason, neither knew how to ask the other about it. So, the question not only went unanswered, it went unasked.

The ride back to the city was uneventful; there was that somewhat depressed mood that often prevails when a vacation is ending, even if it was only a weekend trip. Perhaps it is worse on a short trip. One rides over the same roads that they'd been on just two days earlier, the memory of that happy feeling they'd had on the way out still fresh in their minds.

When they finally crossed over the Hudson into Manhattan, they felt the stifling heat and humidity that they knew had been waiting for them. The weekend was officially over. He made his way down to the lower east side and found a parking spot as close to her building as he could. He carried her bag up the street to her building and they went in. The apartment was empty, Rita wasn't around. He set her baggage down, not sure what to do now, say good bye or take her to bed. She came over and kissed him.

"Thanks, thanks for taking me, thanks for showing me all that. It's been a long time since I got out of town like that. Thanks for everything; I loved every minute of it."

"Well, I was glad to have somebody to go with and I'm glad that somebody was you. So, thank you for coming, thanks...for everything."

"Will I see you Wednesday night, like usual?"

"Try and stop me."

With that he kissed her and left. It was, however, with the feeling the he should have done or said something more. All the uncertainty that he'd thought was left dead and buried up in Saratoga had returned. He couldn't understand what there was about this woman that caused this reaction in him. All he knew was he didn't want to leave her like this, but he'd been worried he would have come off as pushy if he'd tried to stay. Besides, she'd made no attempt to stop him. If Carol had been bothered by his abrupt departure, she never showed it. Their relationship continued on as one might have expected it to. They got together whenever they could, she stayed overnight at his apartment a couple of times, all went well. An idea was quickly growing in John's mind. Within two weeks he'd made his decision.

It was on an afternoon when he knew she was dancing. He stood outside the bar where she was working trying to steady his nerves. He had never come down to see her, had no idea what her act was like or what the place was like for that matter. He took a breath and went in.

It was a dimly lit place, a bar along one wall, tables, and a stage at the far end. Some bad music with a heavy beat was playing loudly. Carol was on the stage, squirming and wriggling to the beat, illuminated by some multi-colored lighting. It all looked pretty harmless actually, her G-string looked like some kind of silky loincloth, tasseled pasties covered her nipples, and she had elastic garters on her stocking tops. It almost seemed like a harmless joke to him. He bought a beer at the bar, then went and sat at an empty table to watch.

After a few minutes, he pulled a dollar bill out of his wallet and folded it in half lengthwise. He went up to the stage, holding the bill up. She didn't recognize him at first, just another customer offering her a tip. She moved to the edge of the stage, then did a double take when she saw who it was. She made a quick gesture, raising her hands, palms upwards at her sides questioningly. He waved the bill back and forth. She smiled her little half smile and extended her leg out. He slipped the bill behind her garter, noting there were several others already there. Then he went back to the table and sat down.

Soon after she finished her set and left the stage, a tall attractive woman approached his table.

"Are you John?" He nodded in response. "OK, Carol said to wait she'd be out as soon as she changes."

He thanked her and watched as she walked away. About fifteen minutes later he saw Carol emerge down by the end of the bar wearing jeans and a tee shirt, her hair now pulled back into its familiar ponytail. She stopped, briefly talking to a man at the bar, then walked away smiling her crooked smile. Another patron turned and said something; she laughed and slapped him on the shoulder. Then, looking around, she spotted John and came over to the table.

"What in the hell are you doing here," her smile had widened, "and why the hell did you only tip me a buck?"

"Just wanted to see where you worked, I'm cheap, and besides that I wanted to ask you something."

"OK, glad to have you, now ask away."

"Ever been to Niagara Falls?"

"No, why, are you planning another weekend trip?"

"Naw, I just always heard it's a good place for a honeymoon."

"Well, yeah, I guess so, it's kind of a traditional thing, isn't it. Why?"

"No particular reason, I just heard it's a good place for a honeymoon. What do you think?"

"Wait a minute, wait a minute," then hesitatingly, "am I hearing you right? Are you, uh, like, proposing to me?"

"Call it what you will, they say the Falls are a great place for a honeymoon. Would you like to see them sometime?"

"Johnny, you've got to be more specific, I'm not sure what you're asking here."

"Well, we could get married, we could just live together, or not; you can stay here and I'll go back to Mackenzie and we can visit each other on weekends, it doesn't matter to me, as long as we're together. So, yes; it's a proposal. It's an unconventional one, but we're not exactly a conventional couple."

"You're serious; I mean this is serious, right?"

He nodded his head. She sat there saying nothing, a blank look on her face. John couldn't help but notice how her age showed at that moment of uncertainty. She appeared tired and worn, not that it mattered to him, in fact he wanted her more than ever.

"Of course, but you have to understand, it can't happen immediately." She spoke slowly, "I had two horrible relationships. John, I know you're not like those two other bastards, but I need time to adjust to the idea, to work this out in my mind before I do it. You understand, don't you?"

"Yes I do." In reality, he didn't, this wasn't the reaction he'd been hoping for. "The offer still stands. I want you to be a part of my life. However you want it, whatever arraignment you're comfortable with is fine with me. I do love you though, understand that."

"I believe you do," she looked up at him, "in fact I'm sure you do. The answer is yes, but I need the time, I can't just jump into this."

She leaned over the table, reached out her arm, hooking her hand behind his neck and pulling him towards her. She kissed him then released him. They both returned to their original positions. Carol's lower lip was trembling slightly as she used the back of her hand to wipe a couple of stray tears from her cheeks.

"We better leave," she said, smiling weakly, "I don't want anyone here to see me like this. The bouncer might think there's something wrong and come over and kick your ass."

"In that case," he stood up, laughing, "Let's get the hell out of here, quick."

"My hero!" Her smile had widened into the one he loved to see.

"Hey, I'm thinking of the bouncer's welfare. I wouldn't want to have to hurt his fist with my face." As they left, Carol turned and waved good bye to the bartender. One or two of the patrons waved back, wishfully thinking she was waving at them.

Later that night, they went with Rita to the girl's favorite bar to celebrate. When they went in, Joe was behind the bar with his usual grumpy look. Seeing them he greeted them good naturedly.

"Hey, Joe," Rita said, "looks like our girl might be leaving us soon."

"Who, Blondie? Where the hell's she goin'?"

"Johnny boy here has swept her off her feet, looks like they're tying the knot."

"About time some fool decided to take her off our Gawd damned hands. Thought she'd never leave." Then, looking at John, "Congrats, buddy, you landed a prize. Grab a booth folks, have a celebration."

They went and sat in one of the booths. Joe came over with three glasses and a bottle of sparkling wine. Setting the glasses down, he removed the wire basket from the neck of the bottle and expertly worked the cork back and forth, finally pulling it so it popped without fly through the air.

"On me, enjoy." He set the bottle down. The wine was a good, sound, domestic champagne. As they drank it, Carol told Rita the story of his proposal.

"It had to be up there with the strangest proposals in the books. In the middle of a strip joint, I'd just finished a set, and he starts talking about a honeymoon at Niagara Falls. He made me figure out what he was talking about." She turned to look at him, "You never did actually ask, just explained."

"Well, you did figure it out. I knew you could." Then he felt Rita's bare foot under the table rubbing on his ankle. He looked over at her but she didn't show any sign of acknowledgement, it was almost as if she didn't realize she was doing it. Later, when Carol went to the ladies room, Rita uncharacteristically stayed behind. Her foot slid up the inside of his leg towards his crotch. He moved as far back in the booth as he could.

"Jesus Christ, Rita, what's wrong with you?"

"Just having a little fun. Remember when we first met? We never did have our night. It's not too late. You could call it an engagement present if you like."

"Damn it Rita, knock it off. Look I know you guys live an unconventional lifestyle, but this is going too far. This isn't going to happen, period."

"Just checking, if you change your mind, just let me know."

"Was this like some kind of a test?"

"Could be, sweetie, I'll never tell."

"OK," Carol said when she returned, "What's been going on here while I was out?"

"I've been trying to seduce John. He's not interested, but I haven't given up yet."

"Keep trying, he might come around."
John wasn't sure what was going on. All he knew was it was an unusual end to an unusual day. He wasn't even sure if he was engaged; he thought he was, but he really wasn't certain.

The uncertainty continued. Carol seemed to be happy he'd asked her, but didn't seem to want to make any plans, or talk about a time frame. He didn't mind if she wanted to wait a year, but he hoped for more than something more specific than vague talk of when she was ready. His summer in New York was drawing to a close and he was looking for an answer. Every time he saw Carol he'd hoped she'd made up her mind. Each time he went over, he'd been determined to find out, but had always let it slide, fearing he'd make her angry and drive her away. Finally one evening he went over to her apartment for a visit and he got an answer the like of which he never expected.

When he arrived, she wasn't ready to go out. That wasn't unusual, she seldom was. As waited, he sort of wandered around the living room, looking at Rita's paintings. Then he noticed a pornographic magazine lying on the coffee table. Curious, he sat down and picked it up, beneath it was an open envelope filled with photographs, several of which had fallen out. He picked up one or two; they were pictures of Carol, at a younger age, engaged in various sex acts.

It was one thing to have been told about these pictures, but it was another thing entirely to see them. A sick feeling ran through him, but he was drawn to the pictures, he couldn't set them down. He flipped through them, in a state of shock. There she was in a variety of positions, sometimes smiling at her partner other times with her face twisted in mock ecstasy, several of her engaged in oral sex. He fought to control his emotions, mixed outrage and disgust. He didn't understand why these damned things had been left here for him to find. He remembered Rita coming on to him at the bar. Were these two incidents some type of sick test? It was then he noticed Carol standing off to the side, nervously looking at him.

"Carol, what in the hell is this shit? Why are they here?"

"I told you about these. I told you they were out there."

"Yeah, but why do you still have them? Why were they left here for anyone to see, for me to see? I don't get it. You and Rita seem to get off playing these fucking games, and I'm getting more than a little sick of them. Now please, please tell me what this is all about."

"My old agent got ahold of me; he thinks he can get me a spread in that magazine.

"OK, OK, I assume you told him no."

Her whole body posture seemed to change. The nervousness was gone as she went on the offensive.

"Who in the hell are you to tell me that? You don't own me. You come here with all your bullshit about loving me, wanting to marry me, and you think that means you're going to tell me how to live my life? I call bullshit on that."

"Your life, no I thought we were talking about

our lives. What the hell Carol, you can't be serious. You can't be considering this."

"You sanctimonious, self-righteous, hypocrite, who in God's name do you think you are?" She was yelling now, "And I thought you were different? Same old shit, different delivery. Instead of hitting, you play mind games, the passive aggressive type."

"Carol, I'm not playing any games here, I'm just trying to…"

"Shut up!" She cut him off. Then picking up one of the photos she held it up. "This is what's got you all upset? It's different when you're the one that's poking me, isn't it? Well, I don't see any fucking difference."

"There's a difference and you know it."

"Yeah, right, as long as I'm putting out for you it's alright, because you came here to save me. That's what it is, isn't it. It's like I'm an old house or a junk car that you decided to fix up anyway you want it to be. No thanks, find yourself another charity case, a different project."

"Carol, it's not like that. Why are you acting like this?"

"Because it's the way I act. Now why don't you get the hell out of here? Go, and don't come back."

He stood looking at her, still bewildered by her outburst, not sure why she had reacted this way. "OK, I'll leave. I'll call you tomorrow, after we've both calmed down."

"Don't bother," was her curt reply. She walked over to the door and opened it slightly, "There'll be no need, just go, for God's sake, go.

She stood by the door, red faced and teary eyed, glaring at him. He walked over pausing in front of her.

"Carol, please don't do this. I don't understand, just…"

"Enough," she shook her head violently, "out!"

She wordlessly jabbed her thumb at the doorway; a silent demand for him to leave. He went out into the hallway, briefly pausing in the doorway to look at her. She shook her head slowly, deliberately this time.

Once he was in the hall, she closed the door behind him. He heard her locking the door behind him.

That's pretty much how it had ended. He walked to the stairs shocked, confused, humiliated, angry, not the least bit sure of what had happened or why she'd exploded in his face. He hoped in the back of his mind that he would run into Rita on the way out, thinking she could help him out or at least give him some insight as to what had happened, but he had no such luck. Once on the street he looked up at the window of her apartment, hoping to see her waving at him to come back. The window was empty.

Every day in the last two weeks he was in the city he debated calling her, hoping to find it had all been a horrible mistake. Then he would remember how bad her outburst had been and decide against it. Finally he convinced himself that there was no point in it. Perhaps it was fear and cowardice on his part or it may have been common sense, either way, when the time came he returned to Mackenzie Academy figuring time would heal all his wounds. And that's how it ended.

5:RESOLUTION

Those were the memories that were running through his mind as the bus pulled into the Port Authority. Up until that moment he'd been sure of what he was doing. Even if it didn't work, he thought of himself as being on a romantic quixotic mission. But now reality was setting in. As he got out of the bus, breathing in the diesel fumed air, the uncertainties all returned. He had no idea how she would react to him and the thoughts of their last meeting began to haunt him.

He remained resolute, however, determined to see it through. If she still didn't want to see him again, so be it. At least he would know and could possibly put it all to rest. He'd come too far now to turn back, besides, he'd rather see an angry Carol then not see her at all and he did want to see her one last time. Once again, he took counsel in the thought that there had to be a reason for Rita to have sent him the picture.

He gathered up his baggage, a suitcase, an overnight bag, and a shopping bag full of presents, and went out to the street. He hailed a cab and rode over to Curt's apartment. When he arrived, Marion greeted him at the door.

"Come on in, John. Curt said you'd be here this afternoon and I should set an extra place for supper. He's at the office, he'll be home later."

"Thanks, Marion," he went in and set his baggage down. He pulled three packages out of the shopping bag.

"I come bearing gifts."

"John, you shouldn't have. I'm afraid we don't have anything for you."

"You're putting me up for a night or two, that's more than enough, especially on such short notice."

"Thank you," she said taking the packages, "I'll put these under the tree. I'm afraid you'll be sleeping on a futon in the other room, it's all we have."

"It'll be more than enough, beggars can't be choosers."

"John, if you don't mind me asking, this is about the girl, isn't it?"

"Yes it is."

"You never did tell us just what happened between you two."

"There's a good reason; there's nothing to tell, simple as that. We had a disagreement, she got mad and told me she never wanted to see me again. I have no idea what it was all about and I've wanted to find out ever since. The holiday break at school seemed like as good a time as any."

"Well, I hope you do find out. Are you thinking about getting back together with her?"

"Only every day for the last four months. I guess it will all depend on what I find when I see her."

"Good luck, then. I hope it works out for you, however you wish."

"Thanks, it's going to be all up to her. Now, I have to ask you if I can use your phone."

"Of course, use the extension in the other room."

He went into the room that would be his home for the next two days. He sat down on the futon and picked up the phone. He hesitated a few moments then dialed the number. Some part of him was wishing nobody would be at home to answer. Somebody was however; there was the clicking as the receiver was picked up and he heard Rita's voice.

"Hello?"

"Rita, hi; it's John Drake. How've you been?"

"Oh, John, this is a surprise! I'm fine, how about you?"

"As good as can be expected. I'm in town for a few days, thought I'd come over and see you guys. Any chance you'll be around tonight?"

"Yes and no, Andre has a thing going on down at the gallery this week, he does it every year at Christmas time. I'll be there and so will Carol. Why don't you drop by? I'd love to see you again. Oh, and John, one other thing."

"What's that?"

"Carol; she's missed you. She won't admit it to you but she has, big time."

"And I her. By the way, I got the picture you sent, thanks."

"Think nothing of it, it just seemed like something you needed. So I'll be seeing you tonight then?"

"I'll be there."

He had a pleasant meal with Curt and his family. They talked mostly about the holidays, past and present. He was thankful nobody pressed him about Carol; he simply wouldn't have known what to say. He really didn't want to explain to anyone about what may well prove to be a fool's errand on his part. The little he'd told Marion was enough, possibly more than enough. Either way, it would have to do for now.

Later that evening he stood in front of the gallery, shopping bag in hand, steadying himself, bolstered by Rita's revelation that Carol had missed him. The place was busy, people were coming and going, some leaving with wrapped artwork. Last minute Christmas shoppers, the reason for this pre-holiday shindig. John had to admire the marketing genius of it all.

Finally he stepped in and looked around. The buffet table was set up in the same place it had been last summer, only this time it was heavier with cookies and other holiday pastries than deli food.

There were two urns one of coffee the other with hot chocolate. Christmas music was playing softly, loud enough to be heard without drowning out any conversation. Then he spotted Rita and made his way over to her.

"John, you made it," she quickly kissed him on the cheek, "I really wasn't too sure you'd come, but I'm glad you did."

"Yeah, well I'm here," he held up the shopping bag, "and I brought you guys some stuff."

"Oh, what have we got?"

"I'm not saying, that's why they're wrapped. I figure you can use the bag to raid the buffet table."

"You're learning, the only trouble is the table's full of cookies and fruitcake. I don't really need too much of them and you can't fill a bag with hot chocolate. It was a good thought though." She grabbed his arm and stared to lead him through the crowd. "Come on, they've got Carol working, she's in the back boxing and wrapping whatever we sell."

As they went towards the back of the gallery, he saw her. She was at a long counter wrapping a framed picture in a generic looking holiday wrapping paper. Her hair was down, like in the picture Rita had sent him. Looking at her, he was amazed at how perfectly Rita had captured her likeness.

"Yo, Carol," Rita suddenly shouted, startling him, "Carol, look who's here. And he brought presents!"

Looking up, she tipped her head to one side and smiled the one-sided half smile that he remembered from the first night. Then she raised her hand and gestured rapidly for him to come over. At least he knew she wasn't hostile. When he got to the counter, her smile widened.

"What brings you here? Have you been in town long?"

He glanced at Rita and she gave him a mischievous little grin. He realized that once again, she hadn't said anything to Carol. This seemed to be a habit of Rita's, springing things on people unannounced.

"Just here for a couple of days, thought I'd drop by and say hello."

She leaned forward over the counter and put a hand on his shoulder, pulling him towards her so she could kiss his cheek. It was the exact type of friendly kiss Rita had given him, friendly and warm, but giving no hint they'd been lovers a few short months earlier.

"Now, did I hear something about presents?"

"Yeah, something here for both of you." He set the bag down, "All yours."

"Looks like two apiece," Rita said, looking into the bag. "This guy's filled with the Christmas spirit. Should we open them now, or wait?"

"Doesn't matter to me, whatever you usually do with Christmas presents."

"Usually,' Carol chimed in, "we say we're going to wait until Christmas when we get them, but open them that same night."

"Well," he said, "who am I to ask you to break with your traditions?"

"How did you know we'd be here, were you

just wandering around the East Side with a bunch of Christmas presents on the off chance you'd bump into us?"

"I have to go back," Rita said distractedly, "there are some people looking at one of my paintings."

Carol watched her friend stroll away. She smiled and shook her head.

"I guess my question was just answered. So, what's new, anything?"

"No, the school's closed for the Christmas break, so I thought I'd come for a visit."

"When did you get in?"

"This afternoon, took the bus."

"You should have let us know."

"Well, it was a spur of the moment decision, besides," he looked at her steadily, "I wasn't sure if you were still mad at me or not."

He wasn't sure if he should have mentioned it or not, but he'd seen no way around it. He saw a look of sadness in her face. She looked down, nervously and then shook her head.

"No, I'm not angry." That was all she said on

the matter. "So, what are you up to? Any plans?"

"Yeah, kind of. I've never been up to Rockefeller Center at Christmas, you know, to see the tree and the skaters. And I've never been inside St. Patrick's. I thought maybe I'd go and check them out."

"I've never been to them either. But why St. Pat's? You never struck me as the religious type, at least you didn't show it last summer."

"I'm not overly religious, but I like the artwork and craftsmanship that went into churches. And there's a majesty to the bigger cathedrals that impresses me. Besides that, people come from all over the world to see it and it's sitting there right under our noses, so I figure I should see it. Anyhow, I don't want to go alone, so, since you've never been, care to accompany me?"

"When are we talking about?"

"Tomorrow morning."

"That means I'll have to get up early," she paused thoughtfully for a moment, "Well, why not? Yes, I'll see you in the morning."

John felt her accepting was a good sign. He was still wary, he'd been wrong about her before and wasn't taking anything for granted.

The next morning he stood with her looking down at the crowd of skaters. It fascinated him that so many could be on the ice at the same time yet nobody seemed to be skating into each other. One girl in particular caught his attention. She was a very good skater, but that wasn't the attraction. It was the way she went about doing jumps and spins seeming oblivious to the presence of the other skaters. It almost seemed to be a typical New York City thing; she'd go into a spin, one leg extended, blade slashing dangerously through the air, while other skaters paid no attention, ducking and dodging their way by her.

"It must be nice," Carol said, "to be that young and carefree. None of them has been burned by life yet, they all probably think the rest of their days will all be as simple as this."

"That's a pretty deep thought. But we were young once too, and we saw things the way they do now. I wish them all well, hope they're always on smooth ice and enjoying themselves." For some reason they were both getting philosophical.

"Oh, don't get me wrong," Carol responded, "I'm not wishing bad luck on them or anything. I'm just jealous, I want to feel the way they do, it's just that I can't anymore."

John had no response, he looked up at the huge Christmas tree, lost in his own thoughts. He did, however, feel the need to say something.

"It's one hell of a tree. I think you'd have to see it at night to really appreciate it though."

He turned and looked at Carol. The chameleon quality of her face constantly amazed him. At times she looked young and vital, other times, like now, she appeared older, tired, and frayed.

"Yes, I suppose so." Then she hesitated, "John, why are you really here? You didn't come all this way to watch people ice skate, now did you?"

"Sure I did, but I also came to see you. You know that, so there's no reason to play these kid's games. The way things ended last summer, that was God awful, I couldn't let it go like that. Not a day's gone by that I haven't thought about you."

"It was terrible," she agreed.

"I had to come back, I had no choice in the matter. I had to see you and talk with you one last time. You have to understand, even if we're no longer a couple, I still want to be your friend. I want more, but I'll settle for that. I still love you, that hasn't changed. I still want to be a part of your life, no matter how small a part it is."

She stood silent, taking his words in. He wondered if he'd spoken out too quickly, putting her on the spot. The last thing he wanted to do was to make her uneasy. He turned and took her by the elbow and looked towards Fifth Avenue.

"Come on, let's go to church."

Crossing the street by the Cathedral they saw a bus in front discharging a tour group. A tour guide led them into the building.

"See what I meant? People from all over come here and neither of us has ever been inside. Now let's go and see what we've been missing."

Once inside, they couldn't help but be overwhelmed by the size and grandeur of the interior. There were several groups of tourist wandering through, pausing to admire the statuary and the side alters. John led her to an empty pew in the back.

"Let's sit for a couple of minutes." His voice was low, slightly above a whisper.

He stepped aside gesturing for her to sit. He watched as she genuflected and crossed herself before side stepping in. She went far enough to leave a place for him before sitting down. He slid in next to her.

"You seem to be the one that's been hiding their religious fervor."

"Oh, that," she whispered back. "I was raised a Catholic; old habits die hard I guess. Besides, when you've lived my life, you need all the help you can get. Hedge your bets and don't offend anyone."

"So, we're both a couple of lapsed Catholics, something else we have in common."

"It seems that way."

"Look, Carol, we have to talk about last summer. Can we do it quietly, you know, no yelling, no anger, just an honest discussion?"

He looked at her waiting for an answer. This was the reason he wanted to talk with her in the back of the cathedral, hoping in such a place there would be little chance of any histrionics on either of their parts; no chance of it escalating into another full blown argument. She sat briefly quiet; her lips pressed tightly together, then bowed her head and slowly nodded.

"Of course, we should, we have to."

"First, I want to say I'm sorry. I'm not sure what I said that set you off, but I sincerely apologize for whatever it may have been. You have to try and understand what it's like for a guy to find out the woman he wants to spend the rest of his life with is going back to the sex trade, to even consider it. I was upset and hurt. If I said anything wrong or hurtful, oh honey, I can't say I'm sorry enough. What you do in this life is up to you."

She leaned forward placing her clasped hands

on the back of the pew in front of them. Her forehead resting on her hands, she looked to any onlookers like she was deep in prayer. In fact, she may well have been.

"It was all a lie, I didn't go back, there was no offer, no agent contacted me. I put those things there deliberately for you to find them."

"So, it really was a test, and I failed miserably."

"No, no test, there was no right or wrong response. I was trying to pick a fight. I wanted to come up with a reason to break up with you."

"But why all the drama?" He was genuinely puzzled now, "Why didn't you just tell me you wanted to break up?"

"Because I didn't want to call it off," her voice wavered, "I felt I had to."

"For God's sake, why? I don't get it. You thought had to, why?"

"I was afraid," she raised her head to look at him, "I was scared, and I was looking for a reason to run."

"What of, me? You needn't have been," he spoke calmly and softly. "Can you explain it? I really want to understand."

Carol sat back in the pew and looked up at the ceiling. He could see she was starting to cry, trying hard to blink back the tears. Then she looked straight ahead and closed her eyes.

"No, I can't, not right now. I don't know how to explain it. Dear God, I've never been so embarrassed or ashamed."

He fished in his pocket and pulled out a handkerchief. He wiped the tears from her cheek with it, then pressed it into her hand.

"Hold on to it, you need this more than I do." He put his hand on her shoulder, "Look, you want to get out of here? We could take a walk up to the park. The fresh air might help and it will give you some time to collect your thoughts. I really have to know what this was all about."

He kissed her on the cheek.

"Don't cry anymore, it's all right, nothing's going to happen. I'm not mad or anything, I just want to come to terms with all this."

"Yes," she nodded her head slowly, "that would be good, thanks."

He slipped out of the pew and stood, waiting to see if she needed help. She moved over and got out, making a quick curtsy towards the main alter. She turned and walked away calmly with him following.

Once on the street, they headed up to Central Park. John put his arm across her shoulders and held her close to him. She didn't say a word for a couple of blocks. Then finally she looked up at him.

"You're too kind. I don't know how you can be so nice to me after what I did."

"I'm still not sure exactly what you did or why and in case you haven't noticed, I've grown kind of fond of you."

"I've noticed. That's why I don't know how to explain it, even to myself."

"Just say what you feel, that's the easiest way."

When they crossed Columbus Circle and headed into the park, Carol went to the first open bench and sat down, John sat next to her.

"OK, it's like this, I was afraid I wouldn't fit in in your world. The closer it came to actually setting a date or making plans, the scarier it got. I guess at the end I was panicking."

"Why didn't you feel you'd fit in?"

"Because; because of what I was, because those pictures still turn up. You never know when or where those loops are being shown. Look, here in the city, nobody knows or cares, you're anonymous, it really doesn't matter what you've done. If somebody were to find out, it simply isn't that big of a deal. You teach at a high class private prep school, if anybody there were to figure it out, what would happen?"

"Not much, I doubt if anyone would find out, and if they did, well it isn't sixteenth or seventeenth Puritan New England, nobody's going to make you wear a scarlet A."

"Not on the outside, but your world is populated by June Cleavers, Carol Bradys, and Aunt Beas. I might not have to wear it, but they'd see the scarlet letter every time they looked at me."

"Who cares what they'd think? I myself have always found that crowd to be very boring."

"It's not only me, what about you? If they were to get on my case, what do you think they'd be saying about you?"

"So you're saying you threw me over for my own good?"

"Yes, sort of."

"First thing is, you're assuming anybody would find out; that's highly unlikely. Second thing, I wouldn't really care what they thought; it's simply nobody else's business. Third, you may be selling these people short; by comparing them to those TV sitcom women you're making the same generalities about them that you think they'd be making about you. Actually, a few that I know would probably be genuinely interested possibly, impressed with it all. Pseudo-intellectuals tend to be liberals. They might even think of you as some kind working class Bohemian heroine."

"Be that as it may, I was terrified. I did what I did. How you must hate me for it."

"No, I don't hate you. I wish you'd have told me all this last summer though. It would have saved me four months of agony."

"You? I cried myself to sleep for weeks. Then I'd get bummed out every time I'd think about it." Then she added defensively, "You really didn't put up much of a fight. I wasn't sure if you really cared. That made it worse."

"I was afraid. I thought if you felt that strongly about it, you'd tear my head off if I argued the point. I mean, you told me not to bother calling you again." He sat up straight and burst out laughing.
"Good God, this is hysterical, we're like two blind mice trying to find our way through a maze, just running around banging into things."

"It's not all that funny."

"The hell it isn't." He quoted a line made popular in the sixties by a movie, "What we have here is failure to communicate."

126

"OK, it's funny, but only after you get past the tears. So, you don't hate me, right?"

"Could never, I told you, I'm still in love with you."

"I just don't see how, but I'm glad to hear it."

"It's like that old saying about if you have something and you let it go, if it doesn't come back then you never really had it, if it does it's yours forever. I came back. I'm still not sure how you feel about it, but I'm yours. If nothing else, like I said before, I'll settle for friendship if that's all you want."

She reached over and took his hand, clutching it tightly in her lap with both of hers.

"I'm glad you're back. I was always hoping you would be, but I was afraid over what you would say if you did."

"And I was afraid of what you would do if I did," he shook his head, smiling. "Are we a couple of fools or what? Instead of being made in heaven, ours was a match made at some clown college."

"I don't care where it was made, as long as it was made somewhere. I'm not going to piss it away again." She leaned against him, "So, where do we go from here?"

"I'd say back where we were before the argument. What's your opinion?"

"I agree. Maybe this whole thing was some kind of blessing in disguise, at least now we know what we've got. I've no doubt about you now, and I hope you've none about me."

"None," he stated simply.

Sitting there John thought about all that had gone on between them; all of it, the ups and the downs. He remembered the first time he'd seen her at the apartment, the first date, and the night they went dancing. Then there was the fight, her throwing him out. It came back to him all too clearly. He thought of the excuses she'd just given him and a troubling thought crossed his mind.

"No, we can't go back to the way it was. It won't work," he shook his head, "it just won't work."

She turned to look at him with a surprised look on her face. Perhaps uneasy would be a better description.

"But I thought we decided to put it all behind us."

"I can't. If we do, the same thing is going to happen. I'm not going to go through this again."

The uneasiness in her face was replaced by anxiety. Her head lowered and he felt her grip on his hand loosen. She appeared to be a beaten woman.

"Look, all of this, this silly assed drama, could have been avoided if you'd told me from the start what was bothering you. We could have talked it out, but you kept it bottled in until it exploded. Look at what we almost lost, all because you didn't let me know what was wrong."

"So, are we about to have another fight?" She was growing defiant.

"I don't think so. The first night I saw you, remember? You busted my chops about being a failed writer. You weren't concerned about hurting my feelings or how I'd react. You just said what you felt. That's the woman I fell for. You were honest, strong, and in charge of your situation. That woman wouldn't have been worried about what some goofy housewives thought about her. That's the woman I want to marry. Can you understand that?"

"You silly bastard, be careful what you wish for, you just might get it." Despite her words, her voice was light hearted.

"Aw, now my cynical friend is back, it's good to see you again." He smiled at her. "Look, this whole 'you fit into my world, I fit into yours' is bullshit. We've got to build our own little world and to hell with the rest of it. You accused me of seeing you as a fixer-upper, but that isn't true. You've had a hard life, and I've been fortunate. I want to share my good luck with you, not to save you or salvage you, but because I love you and I want to be with you. Because there is no woman in my life, and there never has been, even when I was married. It's like I've been waiting for you. That may not make any sense to you, but it's the way I feel."

"No, it makes sense. You're right, this is a conversation we should have had last summer. Now, anything else you've got to say?"

"Yeah, the question you haven't answered. Will you marry me? I mean, it doesn't have to be today or anything, but I want it nice and legal. Like you said, I'm not overly religious, so a wedding in front of a Magistrate will do, but I want you to be my wife, not my girlfriend."

"Of course," she stated matter of factually. One of her hands released its grip on his and, moving to his cheek, turned his head towards her. She kissed him softly.

"Try and stop me from marrying you. You can set the date, any time you want."

"June is a nice time, kind of traditional, and I'm a traditional kind of a guy."

Apprehensive Hearts

"A June bride; that sounds lovely." A second kiss.

"Another thought," he whispered, "it's not too late to catch a bus back to Mackenzie, you could spend Christmas at your future home. The faculty and staff do the holiday up pretty big. A Christmas Eve party, a dinner Christmas day, it's all kind of free flowing, with people coming and going as they please. It'll be a good chance for you to meet the blue nosed old biddies that had you so spooked. I think you'll find they're not really such a bad lot. That is, unless you'd rather not leave Rita alone on Christmas."

"She'd probably be glad to get me out of her hair. You know, she was pissed when I broke up with you. She was planning on having her boyfriend move in and I screwed that all up on her. I don't think she appreciated it."

"Don't sell her short honey. I think she's a better friend than that. Maybe she knew what was best for us even if we didn't."

"Well, we might as well head back so I can start packing. Now, how about New Years, can we spend that in the city? I know where to go for a good party."

"Sounds like a fair exchange. Now let's go and get this show on the road."

When they stood up, Carol turned and looked at him for a moment, then suddenly threw her arms around him, pulling him firmly against herself, clinging to him her head resting against his chest. He was surprised by it all; surprised that it happened and surprised that so thin a woman had so strong a grip. His upper arms were held in place by her embrace, all he could do was raise his forearms and hold her around the waist. She was pressed tightly enough that he could feel her breathing and noticed there was a ragged, irregular quality to it.

"Carol," he asked quietly, "are you crying?"

"Uh-huh," she answered affirmatively.

"For God's sake, why?"

"Because," she replied without lifting her head, "because I'm glad; glad you came back, glad we're going to get married, glad I'm going away with you tonight, and even glad I'll be meeting your friends and I don't care what they think of me. I'm also glad I never told you how much I love you. I've used the word, but I never told you how much. I'm glad I never told you, because now I get to tell you for the first time here and now in the most appropriate time and place. I love you Johnny Drake, with all my heart."

With that her grip loosened slightly as she lifted her head and leaned back slightly looking up at him. Her cheeks were wet with tears as she tried to smile.

"Do you know why I never told you that before?" She watched as he shook his head slowly. "I didn't tell you because I was afraid I'd ruin it, jinx it somehow. I was attracted to you from that first date at the steakhouse. Then that time we went dancing, I could tell you weren't big on dancing but you went anyhow, just for me. How could I not love you?"

She laid her head against his shoulder again. "Every time I told you something else about my past I expected you to run, but you didn't. Then there was Saratoga. That night when you said you loved me, guys say things like that all the time when their trying to get a woman into bed or to keep them in bed, or want to be sure they'll come back to their bed, but you said it when you thought I was asleep and wouldn't hear you. I knew then that you meant it and I thought I was the luckiest girl in the whole damned world, but I still was afraid to tell you. Even that day at the club when you proposed to me, that beautifully lovely, goofy proposal; it brought me to tears, but even then I couldn't tell you."

"You've told me now," he told her, "that's all that counts."

"No, I want to be sure you understand. I was afraid of getting hurt, of being disappointed. Remember, my ex used to accuse me of tricking him into marrying him, I guess I was afraid of that happening again, afraid I'd scare you off if I pressed it. Then I was afraid your friends would ruin it on me if they ever found out about my past. So I did what I did, and you still came back for me. That's the best Christmas present I ever could have gotten, thank you. I love you Johnny Drake, more than you'll ever know."

"Now," she continued, "you said we should be open with each other and not hide our feelings. That's what I'm doing now so we can start with a clean slate."

Taken aback by her words, John could think of nothing to say. He held her for a few moments before speaking.

"Come along, my love," he said gently, "let's go to the Port Authority, check the schedules and get our tickets. We have a Christmas Party to go to and it's a long way from here."

Carol looked up at him, nodded her head, and kissed him one more time. Stepping back, she took his hand in hers and pushed both into her coat pocket for warmth as they walked down the street.

Later that evening, he sat talking with Rita at the apartment while he waited for Carol to finish preparing for their trip. For once he was completely at ease and self-assured. Carol's speech in the park had bolstered his confidence. There was no longer any doubt in his mind about her or their relationship, any problems they might have from here on would be merely bumps in the road; nothing they couldn't overcome. So many times he'd thought that last summer, but now he knew it.

"I hope I haven't ruined your holiday," he said looking at Rita, "you know, taking Carol away like this."

"No, not at all, you think this didn't cross my mind when I first suggested you two should get together way back in the beginning? It's quite all right," she assured him, "I'm just glad to see Carol so happy for once. That's what it's all been about."

He sat quietly for a moment, lost in the thought that he'd been right, Rita was a better friend than Carol had realized. Then, as he looked at her, she raised one finger in the air indicating for him wait. She got up and went over to some canvases that were leaning against the wall and picked one up.

"I want your opinion on this one while you're here. I based it on what Carol told me about your description of what you'd seen on that mountaintop up North. I don't know if I got it right, since it was based on third hand information."

She held it up in front of her for him to see. It was a view of mountain peaks rising out of a low lying cloud bank into a sunny sky.

"I'm calling it 'Islands in the Sky'. It's not the

Adirondacks, just a sort of Bob Ross generic mountain scene, but does it look realistic to you?"

"Yes, it does. You've captured the essence of it. You're pretty good at doing that sort of thing actually."

"Thanks, I really like this one myself. I'm thinking of having some prints made of it. If I do, I'll give you guys one as a wedding present."

"That would be nice. You know that picture of Carol that you sent me; you portrayed her better than any photograph ever could. A matter of fact, that's what brought me back here yesterday."

"Thanks again, I'm glad I could help out. After all, remember, that first night when we talked about her," she gave him a quick wink and a smile, "I told you then I didn't think you'd do it on your own."

He nodded his head slowly in agreement, she had been right and he was grateful for her interference. Before he could answer, Carol came out of the bedroom dragging two suitcases.

"I hope I'm not taking too much," she said, "I'm not really sure what I'll be needing, so I might have gone a bit overboard."

"Better to take too much than not enough, sweetie," Rita answered.

"Yeah," John agreed, "take as much as you want, don't worry about it. If you're ready though, I'll give Curt a call."

It was another imposition on his friend, Curt had agreed to come down and drive them to the bus terminal. He got up and made the call. Once he hung up he came back and sat down.

"He said he'd be here in about twenty minutes. That gives you guys plenty of time for good-byes."

"You make it sound like she's leaving forever," Rita said, "it's just a couple of days."

"Yes," Carol added, "and Rita's one of those rare, hard to find things in this world; a friend for life. So even after we get married, we'll be in touch and don't be surprised if she comes to visit us every now and again."

"I wouldn't have it any other way," John agreed, "Remember, I owe her something too."

"You may not realize it," Carol explained, "but when we first met, about ten years ago, I'd already straightened myself out, but I was struggling to stay straight. I might not have made it if it weren't for her. You don't forget a thing like that and you don't lose a friend like that."

"Enough of this mush," Rita said in mock distain, "shouldn't we wait outside for your friend?"

"Yes, I believe so," John said as he looked at his watch, "he should be here soon."

When they all got up, John picked Carol's bags off the floor, carried them down stairs, and out on the stoop. As they stood waiting, the women chatted idly while John stared at the stone step. He was thinking about the night last June when he and Rita had stood here waiting for the cab and she had first talked to him about going out with Carol. He remembered nervously walking up them the night of their first date and also the horrible feeling when he walked down them the night in August when she threw him out. He had a lot of history with this stoop.

Finally Curt's station wagon pulled up in front of the building and double parked. Marion quickly emerged from the passenger side, half running across the sidewalk and up the steps. She brushed by him on her way up as he came down with Carol's luggage.

"I have to congratulate her," she murmured as she passed.

When he reached the sidewalk, John turned around and looked up. Carol and Marion were embracing each other. The air was filled with the giggling laughter of all three women. Curt was standing at the back of his vehicle opening the tailgate. As John approached him he grabbed one of the suitcases and slid it into the back, then stepped aside as John swung the other up and into the wagon. While Curt closed the tailgate, John looked at the three women on the stoop.

"What do you suppose they're talking about?" he asked Curt.

"You; have you forgotten what it's like when you're married? When you can't hear what they're saying but can hear them laughing, they're usually talking about you."

John nodded and shook his head, smiling laconically. He then crossed the sidewalk, and headed for the stoop. Ascending the steps, he paused before speaking.

"I hate to break it up, but I have to." He put a hand on Rita's shoulder kissed her cheek, "We'll see you for New Year's, kid."

"I'll be waiting," she said and kissed him back.

"Well," he said turning to Carol, "it's that time, sweetheart. Let's go home."

Carol stood still for a moment, her eyes were closed and the smile on her face seemed frozen in place. Briefly, John wondered if she was having second thoughts about it all. Then she opened her eyes and looked at him, flashing the good smile, the beautiful one that he loved to see.

"You don't know how much I wanted to hear that."

"What," he asked, "you mean me calling you sweetheart?"

"No," she said, "home, you said 'Let's go home'. After twenty three years, I'm finally going home."

He watched as Rita put her hand on Carol's shoulder and shook it slightly and then kissed her friend on the cheek in a congratulatory gesture. Then she looked past Carol at John and nodded her head in wordless approval. Marion was standing on the bottom step looking up, her lips pressed tightly together in a strange somewhat pained looking smile, trying to suppress her emotions. She was obviously moved, either by Carol's words or Rita's action.

He felt a strange sensation within himself. It was a blend of feelings; delighted that she seemed this happy, pride that he was the source of it, and relief that the months of uncertainty, anxiety, and turmoil had ended well. She had been worth every agonizing moment of it. Even the argument and four months without her had served a purpose, without it they wouldn't have had their earlier heart to heart talk up in Central Park. It had been the broom that had swept the clutter of the past out of their lives. Now they understood each other.

He was determined to make the rest of her life as blissful as he could. Raising his elbow, he offered her his arm. When she took it, sliding her hand through it, he felt like a groom posing on the church steps with his new bride. The few light snow flakes drifting down on them seemed like nature's way of throwing rice on some newlyweds. He knew then their actually wedding day would be anticlimactic compared to this moment.

"Twenty three years," he said reflectively, looking at her, "then it really is time for you to come home. You've been out in the cold far too long, my love."

They descended the stairs arm in arm and walked towards Curt's car and their future, together.

ABOUT THE AUTHOR

About the Author
A lifelong member of the working class, Vietnam veteran, bookbinder, warehouseman, retail worker, and laborer with a passion for good times, laughter, old cars, cold beer, Nordic skiing, and nature.

I am most at home with the ordinary people of this world. The ones that interest me are the ones who have taken a few hard knocks in life and come up laughing. They are the ones who don't run from the rain, accepting that they are going to get wet and feel it's all a part of the journey; in other words the common clay that is the foundation of this world. These are the people I love and the ones I choose to write about.

OTHER WORKS
Apprehensive Hearts
My Brother's Keeper – a boxer's story
Walking Away – a life in flux